INbOX

Where the secret lies

Pen Writes

Cover Design: Maurice Ingram and Men-Tal

Published by G Publishing LLC

Library of Congress Control Number: 2019918935

ISBN: 978-1-7340865-1-5

Printed in the United States of America

Snatched

Sometimes the strength of one's terror is wild enough to make another's most savage nightmares feel like a lullaby…

Her eye sluggishly blinked as she was slowly coming to. Gradually regaining consciousness her thinking was cloudy ***What's happening?*** The pain in her face…and in her rib cage caused her to wince intensely. Her left eye throbbed tremendously and felt very puffy and swollen; barely able to open. Breathing faster she immediately realized something was fucking wrong! Her hands were bound together behind her back inescapably! Her ankles were duct taped as well slowly cutting off her circulation! Her eye widened as she frantically looked around but could see nothing! ***What the fuck?! God No, what's going on?!*** She could hear the trunk rattle as they drove over a bump. Immediately she knew she was being abducted. She started crying and frantically kicking and squirming trying to break lose! Mucus slowly filled in her nostrils making it harder to breathe! Only she could hear her faint moans as she started weeping hopelessly. She tried looking down ***What the fuck am I wrapped in***. She prayed for some type of miracle in her mind and tried calming down so she could breathe better. ***Who the fuck could be kidnapping me!! Did I do something to someone? Did he owe somebody some money? Did he get into some type of drama with somebody?! Did he kill somebody and they holding me for ransom or revenge? What the fuck is going on?!*** Only thing she could vaguely recall was a violent punch to the face. She felt the car slowing down a little and make a slow shaky turn. The car drove slowly, came to a stop and parked. She was scared as fuck as she listened closely. Her heart pounded even harder once she heard two car doors open and shut. She hoped someone could just hear or see her and call for help! She struggled intensely to break loose but suddenly she stopped. She could feel her heart thump harder than ever as she tried to remain silent and just listen. She tried to catch their muffled voices but couldn't quite make out what they were saying. She slightly heard footsteps getting closer. She heard the latch pop and then the trunk lifted. She tried to scream her ass off and squirm as they lifted her. She tried to guess who the hell was out to get her. She heard what sounded like something smashing or being kicked open and she tried breaking lose again!!! She heard one of them say ***Let's hurry the fuck up! Toss this bitch down there!*** She felt them swing her once and then heaved her in the air. Her helpless body BANGED hard as hell down the flight of stairs; she was petrified. It felt like she got hit in the head with a bowling ball as she slammed against the cement basement floor. She started moaning and crying; felt like the corner of a stair cracked a rib! Tears streamed from her eyes as she started hyperventilating. She just wanted to go home to her family. Squirming intensely to break free because she was suffocating!... She heard the door shut and then footsteps coming down the stairs. Suddenly she heard a couple of click clack sounds. ***Oh my God please don't let them****....* Immediately multiple rounds of gunshots were let off piercing her legs and torso! She flinched with every hit as her heart began sputtering into a cardiac arrest. ***Oh My God!!*** One more shot fired; that bullet pierced through her skull...

Behind the Yellow Caution Tape

October 4th 2019 – 8:37 am - Friday morning – Detroit Michigan's Westside. It was the normal daily routine for Detective Melvin Price and his partner Detective Ms. Valencia Stevenson. He stroked his goatee as he thought deeply. They looked around as they swiftly whipped up on a crime scene and parked. Valencia took off her baseball cap and then took a rubber-band out of her pocket. She put her beautiful shoulder length hair in a ponytail and put her hat back on; she was good to go. It was cold and brisk with a little snow on the ground. Yellow caution tape quarantined the area and numbered markers on the pavement identified anything that can possibly be used as evidence.

"You think we'll see anything new?" Detective Valencia asked.

Detective Melvin chuckled and replied "What haven't we seen?... Just try not to throw up if we do."

"I got a rock gut and no gag reflex; I don't throw up." Valencia replied as they got out of the all black squad car.

They walked towards the house and stepped under the caution tape. Detective Melvin had a camera hanging from his neck by its tassels and they both wore latex sterile gloves. They headed to the backyard where the entry took place. They noticed the clasp had been ripped off the hinge; a sign of forced entry. Melvin grabbed his camera and took a picture of the broken hinge. Upon entry there was a small landing and a staircase that led downstairs to the basement. Detective Valencia noticed a slender sliver of wood slightly sticking out from the wall. She then noticed a small ripped piece of fabric stuck on it like maybe from a jacket or a T-shirt. Detective Melvin took a picture of it and then stepped inside. Detective Valencia carefully grabbed the sliver and easily managed to get it loose from the door entrance along with the fabric attached to it. She placed it inside of a plastic sandwich baggie and then placed it inside of a brown paper bag which holds any evidence. To their right was a step that led up to the kitchen. At the bottom of the staircase was a green tarp like material or sheet stained with what looked like blood and a body wrapped in it. They looked closer and noticed it was a leg hanging out of it with the foot propped up on the stair. At the other end it looked like the top of a woman's head peering out of the tarp. Blood stained the forehead where the bullet entered. Melvin snapped a couple more pictures as they carefully stepped down the stairs. By it being cool outside the body wasn't decomposed and there weren't any maggots yet; just a few flies and gnats buzzing around the corpse.

"Looks like a woman wrapped in a tarp and perhaps tossed down these stairs." Detective Melvin said, judging by the marks on the wall and the hair sticking out.

"Yeah, and it looks like she was shot multiple times. The suspect or suspects may have burst in, tossed her down the stairs, possibly shot off some rounds from up there on the landing to make sure she was dead and fled the scene." Detective Valencia suggested.

"Maybe…or maybe not." Detective Melvin replied as he stood on the third stair from the bottom and pointed at a half-smoked cigar lying on the stair and took a picture of it.

Valencia carefully grabbed the cigar and placed it in its own plastic baggie and then placed it in the brown evidence bag. They both carefully stepped over the body and glanced around the basement. He took a picture of the body and another picture of the foot on the stair.

"Hmmm... close range?" Valencia asked as they carefully stepped around the body.

Detective Melvin took a picture of the blood splatter on the wall then bent down and looked closer.

"Yeah I think so. If you look at the way the blood is splattered and projected on the wall it can help you determine the proximity of the shooting. And this looks like a close-range shooting." Detective Melvin answered, analyzing the blood drops.

They carefully pulled back the tarp uncovering the body and Melvin immediately took pictures. The side of her face and body were soaking in blood. He snapped a few pictures of her swollen black eye and the duct tape covering her mouth. He also snapped multiple pictures of the duct tape that bound her hands together behind her back. There was a piece of duct tape still in a circular shape stuck on her left foot and he snapped a picture of that as well. It was also visible that she was shot multiple times; twice in the face, five times in the torso and once in the leg.

"It looks like her feet were bound together and she managed to kick loose. That's how her right foot was able to be on the stair." Detective Valencia said.

"For some reason I'm just guessing it was more than one person involved. From what I hear, the neighbors say they hadn't seen anything or heard anything which is kind of hard to believe. No one heard any fighting, screaming or gun shots. The door was forced open and nobody seemed to have heard that. I WANT ANSWERS…because this shit isn't making any fucking sense! You got neighbors that live right next door, and across the street and no one heard any gun shots." Detective Melvin said emphatically.

"Perhaps there was a silencer on the gun." Detective Valencia threw out there.

Detective Melvin thought for a second and then shook his head. "This wasn't a professional job. A professional wouldn't have left a fabric tear on the entry of the door. I guarantee you there's clues in this tarp and on this duct tape. I want a scan ran on that fabric you got off the door. I want to know what brand of clothing that it came from and what stores it's sold in. I want to know every time this piece of clothing was sold; was it with cash or credit and if it was credit then I want a printout of all of those who purchased it with a credit card. I want a DNA trace on the sliver of wood it was on. I want a DNA trace ran on the cigar and see if it matches anyone in our criminal database. I want to know who the fuck this murderer is!" Detective Melvin said passionately.

"Melvin…calm down we're going to find who did this. I got faith in us…I believe in you." Detective Valencia replied.

Moonlight at the Riverwalk

Sunday – September 8th, 2019 – Downtown Detroit – 8:45pm.

Moonlight spilled across the dark rippling water of the Detroit River so beautifully. The night breeze felt fantastic as Peaches and Antonio eased up the walkway. Antonio was very attracted to Peaches, he adored her butter-pecan complexion, sexy eyes and plump glossy lips. Peaches loved how his well-groomed big beard faded off going towards his scalp. Casually they greeted another couples in passing; it was a beautiful feeling. The night was the type of night a person would love to enjoy for the rest of their lives.

"Tonight just feels so fantastic!" Peaches expressed happily as she twirled around with her arms stretched out embracing the night breeze.

"I knew a trip down here would make you feel really good." Antonio said.

"Yes it did. I wish every night could be like this." Peaches replied, smiling looking up at his tall six foot tall caramel frame.

"One day…it's coming, one day." Antonio said, stopping by the huge stones that led down into the river.

"I need you to make that one day really soon; I need this in my life." Peaches slides her arm around Antonio's waist and looks out over the water.

"I'm working on it right now. I love to see your beautiful face under the chardonnay moon." Antonio said, looking up at the moon.

"Don't be trying to run them poetic lines on me." Peaches responded, loving what he was saying.

"I ain't just saying it, I mean it. These types of moments are so beautiful to me. I absolutely love the nature, the water, the cool breeze, the darkness, the stars, the reflection of the moon." Antonio said, gazing at the sky.

"You're so deep. Why you just didn't call it moonlight?" Peaches asked.

"Because the moon is not a light." Antonio answered, gazing at the moon.

Peaches glanced at the moon and looked back at him and asked. "Well how is the light beaming down from the moon if it isn't a light?"

"Because the moon reflects the light from the sun to the earth." Antonio answered, smiling at her.

"So you're telling me that's not a light I'm looking at?" Peaches asked.

"Let me ask you this. Have you ever seen a light shine half of itself?" Antonio asked.

"No because it can't." Peaches answered.

"Exactly because no matter what side of a light you stand on you will always see the whole light as it is. You never see half of a light, but…you definitely can see a half moon." Antonio expressed.

"Wow now that makes sense. I never thought about it like that." Peaches smiled.

"Think about this. How would we explain a three-quarter moon or half-moon if the moon was a whole light?" Antonio asked.

"Tell me." Peaches said, loving his intelligence.

"Well the phase of the moon we see depends on the angle the sunlight is hitting it. For instance, hold your finger up." Antonio said.

Peaches held her index finger straight up and Antonio pulled out a lighter from his pocket and lit it about an inch and a half away from her finger.

"Okay let's say this fire is the sun. Do you see how your finger is more bright on one side and more darker on the other side?" Antonio asked

"Yes." Peaches answered, looking at her finger.

"And if I move the light around you'll start to see different parts of your finger that's lit and the side that's shaded. That's exactly how the phases of our moon works as the sun shines on it." Antonio said.

"Wow the most sexiest shit is an intelligent man…with a beard." Peaches said, touching his beard.

"Oh so what's going to happen when I cut this beard off?" Antonio asked, laughing.

"Um I'm leaving yo ass; don't play." Peaches replied.

"Damn for real?" Antonio laughed.

"Leave the damn beard alone. You hear me?" Peaches replied, twirling her fingers through it.

"Damn what's more important me or the beard?" Antonio asked, amused by her silliness.

"Well um…let's see…the beard…and then you. It actually goes hand in hand; can't have one without the other." Peaches expressed.

"Really?" Antonio leaned back with his mouth open and eyes wide being silly.

"How can I put it to you?... This kittycat without that beard is like having a flower without sunlight and water; it ain't happening. It's a biological necessity." Peaches explained, smiling.

"Wow, you literally have a scientific breakdown for beards. Yo ass is crazy; some type of beard psycho." Antonio shook his head and laughed.

"Yes crazy and psycho enough to surgically slice all of your little clipper cords into so many tiny pieces you will think it was a trail of ants crawling on the floor." Peaches said.

"Oh you crazy crazy." Antonio said.

"Now since you are inquiring about cutting shit off; what you can cut off is them hoes." Peaches replied, putting her hand on her hip.

"Hoes? What am I going to do about you? Ain't nobody got no hoes, woman." Antonio said, shaking his head.

"Whatever Tony, I see all the little subliminal comments women leave on your page and pics. Then you keep your phone locked with some type of encrypted Da Vinci code. You think I don't know what's up with them extra strength passwords and locks on your phone? It means you got the hoes." Peaches replied.

"You know what, I almost forgot. You will create a monster in your own mind just to run from it." Antonio grabs her hand and holds it.

"You think that?" Peaches asked.

"Babe yes I think that, you're a commitment-phobe." Antonio glanced at the people on the Detroit Princess boat cruising by.

"I'm not a commitment-phobe I just have a low tolerance for bullshit. If I think I see something then yes I will run." Peaches replied, looking up at him.

"Trust me, you're a commitment-phobe." Antonio replied.

"Whatever." Peaches replied, pushing him playfully.

"Babe...there are no hoes okay, I have no hoes." Antonio assured, compassionately caressing her arms.

"No hoes?" Peaches asked.

"No hoes." Antonio answered.

"...Okay...I trust you..." Peaches said, looking down.

"Babe, look at me; I need you to trust me like for real." Antonio replied, looking in her eyes.

"Okay...I'm trying...I do." Peaches nodded her head.

Antonio slowly pulled her to him and wrapped his arms around her and kissed her forehead. His hug felt so warm and loving to her. She wrapped her arms around his waist, closed her eyes and rested her head on his chest. She always fantasized of that Knight in shining Armor or that hero to rescue her and make her happy for the rest of her life. She wanted to trust him but honestly still felt a little unsure. She'd been through a lot of heartbreaks and disappointment in her life. She thought about how she felt about Antonio and smiled.

"Babe we gone get ready to jet in a moment because my ass gotta be up early for work in the morning." Antonio said, pulling her to him.

"Okay." Peaches replied as they kissed.

HOME

MONDAY – SEPTEMBER 9TH, 2019 – 6:16PM – ANTONIO'S HOUSE. Peaches grabbed a wine glass from the cabinet and went to the sink to rinse it out. She went to the fridge and grabbed a bottle of wine and poured almost a full glass. She sat the bottle down and took a sip; leaning her back up against the counter. She dried her hands off on the dish towel and grabbed her cellphone out of her pocket. She went on her social media page and started scrolling not noticing anything unusual, just the same ole shit. She shook her head as she looked at her feed ***I swear some of these people need to get a life.*** She sipped her wine again and continued scrolling and clicking like on certain pictures she saw. A little inbox circle dropped down on her screen and she clicked on it. ***Oh my God, I'm so sick of niggas and this hello Queen shit. At least if you're going to say it be one of those woke niggas.*** She rolled her eyes, and downed her drink. She poured herself some more and clicked on her inbox icon to see the rest of her messages. She clicked a few inboxes and was very turned off by the nerve of some dudes. ***Wow dick pic, dick pic, after dick pic. At least if you're going to send a damn dick pic have a nice-looking dick to look at. Ain't nobody ask for your lame dick.*** She clicked on another message and her eyes scrunched in disbelief as she read what a guy messaged her. ***I will pay you one hundred dollars to send me a picture of your feet. I also have a pair of panties I want you to put on and wear them for a week straight and I'll pay you one-thousand dollars.*** Her mouth fell open flabbergasted by what she just read. ***Wow these muthafuckas are crazy. He really wants to pay me so he can sniff my pussy and ass through my panties.*** She shook her head, sipped more of her drink as she slowly scrolled. This one particular dude named Dough Boy, who always sends her random annoying inboxes, sent her another one. His distorted profile pic looked so weird, creepy and stalker-ish. He is all over the place with the things he says in her inbox and she was just about to block him. Abruptly her phone rung and she answered it.

"Wsup Girly, what you doing?" Niya asked.

"Nothing, just scrolling on Facebook and sipping me some wine." Peaches answered lamely.

"Oh okay...you okay? You sound a little bit irritated." Niya pointed out.

"Girl, I'm just so sick of Facebook, Instagram, Twitter, Back Page, Front Page and all this other dot com social media bullshit these niggas be on. I think I'm going to just deactivate my pages and just do me for a while." Peaches answered, exhaling.

"Damn, what happened to make you want to shut your pages down? Did something happen with you and Antonio?" Niya asked.

"I'm just sick of all the lil groupie hoes and all the photo likes and slick ass lil comments and shit. I don't trust these little bitches and all these smiley faces and heart eyes and shit. Asking him do he still do manicures and massages. You know all that little bullshit talk they think you don't catch onto. And I ain't stupid, I already know bitches all up in his fuckin inbox sending him naked pics and God knows what. I just don't want to deal with it anymore." Peaches said as she eased into the living room.

"I mean is he saying something disrespectful to these women? Have you ever caught him messing around with one of them?" Niya asked.

"No but I aint about to set myself up to believe he aint and get played either. If he want these hoes he can have them." Peaches said, looking at a picture of Antonio and herself on the mantel piece.

"Ima be honest with you, it sounds like you're pissed off based off what's going on in your inbox and applying it to your relationship. You never said he was trying to get on the women; you said the women trying to be slick and get at him." Niya said, trying to be a voice of reasoning.

"I hear you but I aint trying to hear that right now. I just feel the way I feel; call me irrational I don't care." Peaches looks out the window, hearing a car pull up.

"Look, I aint trying to tell you what to do but I hope you and Antonio can settle down with each other. It's too much shit going on out here and you don't know who to trust. STDs is running rampant, women and men on the down low and you can barely tell them apart nowadays. And I know you know about all the sex trafficking and black women that's been coming up missing here in Detroit." Niya said.

"Yeah I heard about that strange white van and the kidnappings." Peaches replied.

"Exactly that's what I'm saying." Niya emphasized.

"Yeah…well…he just pulled up so Ima um, call you tomorrow." Peaches said, walking back in the kitchen.

"Okay, talk to you tomorrow. And just think about what I said to you." Niya said.

"Niya, bye, I love you, I'll talk to you tomorrow, good night." Peaches said, grabbing the bottle of wine and pouring herself the last of it.

"Okay meanie, I love you too. Talk to you tomorrow." Niya replied.

Peaches hung up the phone and sat it down on the counter. She leaned back with her arms crossed and sipped her wine. She could hear Antonio's keys jingle as he unlocked the door and opened it. He stepped in and shut the door behind him. To his happy surprise he noticed Peaches leaned up against the kitchen counter.

"Hey babe, what you doing?" Antonio asked.

"...Nothing." Peaches barely uttered.

"What's wrong? You don't seem pleased right now... These are for you." Antonio said, pulling flowers out of a bag and lying them down on the counter.

Peaches barely looked at the flowers and replied, "Thank you."

"O...kay can you please tell me what's wrong?" Antonio asked, starting to get frustrated because he knows she's lying.

"I said nothing." Peaches answered with an attitude.

"Didn't you say you don't like somebody lying to you? But you gone sit here and lie to me? Antonio asked, tired of the double standards and mind games.

"Antonio go take those smelly work clothes off; it's irritating." Peaches said, irritated look on her face.

"You know what? Fuck it, don't talk; stay fucking mute then." Antonio said and walked off headed upstairs.

Peaches waited till he almost got to the stairs and said "Tell all yo little fuckin hoes to stay fucking mute."

Antonio stopped in his tracks for a second and then turned around. He mildly walked back into the kitchen. "Peaches, what the hell are you talking about?"

"You know what the fuck I'm talking about? Don't play dumb." Peaches answered, slight frown on her face.

"If I knew what the fuck you were talking about I wouldn't be asking you what the fuck you're talking about. Now why don't you stop playing the emotional fucking mind games and just be clear about what it is that you're talking about so we can REASONABLY resolve this shit." Antonio replied.

"You know what?... Since I'm playing emotional fucking mind games go talk to your little hoes and ask them what's wrong with me." Peaches replied, nonchalantly sipping her wine.

"You know fucking what?! I've been busting my muthafuckin ass to take care of us all muthafuckin day. I happily come home and bring you flowers to put a fuckin smile on your face. Then you can't even give me the respect to reasonably talk to me about what the fuck it is that's troubling you? I gotta deal with stupid ass coworkers all fuckin day. I gotta worry about if I am going to make it home as a black man without the police killing me… Only thing I want to have when I walk through my door is a peace of fuckin mind; that's it." Antonio eloquently preached.

Peaches paused for a moment and replied "You know what? I want peace too…and a break."

Antonio just looked at her. "So what the fuck is that supposed to mean? A break?"

"Exactly what I said, a fuckin break." Peaches replied.

“A break? Translation, you just want time to go out and fuck with other niggas. Ima tell you right now I’m not that lame ass nigga that will accept that. It’s too much shit out here and I ain’t trying to catch shit. Not a drip, not a burn, not A.I.D.S, not none of that shit.” Antonio said with a mean scowl on his face.

“I never said that! I never said I wanted time to fuck with other niggas. I said I need a break, space. You want me to be clear and spell it out? S.P.A.C.E, space.” Peaches replied, frustrated by life.

“Well you know what? You can have your fuckin S.P.A.C.E. End of fuckin Discussion.” Antonio said and walked off.

Peaches just stood there leaned up against the counter with her hand over her face shaking her head.

AFTER WORK AFFAIR

Thursday – September 12th, 2019 – 3:30pm. It was an annual party at the Quick and Loans Company. The music was hype and the place was wall to wall with employees and friends drinking and mingling. A few tables were set up full of delicious food from chicken, steak, macaroni, greens etc.; had people's mouths watering. They had a small area off to the side where people were able to dance and get their hustle on. A group of women were out on the dance floor putting on a show dancing with each other. Some of the fellas stood around with their drinks in their hands and admired the sexy ladies looking good bouncing ass from left to right. Over on the other side of the room Peaches was standing around with a group of coworkers having a random discussion about a Facebook post. It was Peaches close friend Tangie who was reading from her phone about a post that was made in one of the groups she's in. Tangie was tall, five-eleven, thick and shaped nice. She had a short bob haircut, and a pretty brown skinned face.

"Okay, this first question I want to ask is from a very good friend of mine post. Her name is Kim Carter, she host a show called Kicking It With K and she talks about a lot of different subjects that pertain to our lives." Tangie said.

"Okay, come on with it." Bernard said, taking a gulp of his drink.

"Okay, first question. One of my favorite questions to ask until us ladies get answers." Tangie said.

"Aw shit, here we go." Bernard said, being sarcastic.

"Anyway, be quiet. Okay question, why do all men cheat?" Tangie looks up and around at everybody seeing who wants to answer first.

"Aw hell nall, we might be on Candid Camera. I'm out of here fellas." Bernard laughed, shaking his head.

"Don't be shaking your head; this is real shit. Don't get scared, just answer the damn question." Peaches said, laughing.

"Men cheat simply because they just flat out want to cheat. They want their cake and eat it too and they really don't give a fuck about the woman that they're with or hurting." Danielle answered.

"I'm feeling what Danielle just said. I think men just cheat simply because the opportunity is there and they don't care to hold themselves to a high standard of fidelity." Tangie added.

"Right! Like they have a very low standard for themselves." Danielle replied.

"I think men are insecure creatures and want their ego stroked by other woman." Peaches said.

"Bernard, why do you cheat?" Tangie asked, putting him on blast.

Bernard laughed for a second and looked at Tangie. "Damn you just automatically know I cheat huh?"

"Boy answer the damn question." Tangie replied, laughing.

"Damn well um, I cheat because I get bored with being faithful. The excitement is gone and I want to feel that height of excitement; that shit feels good. Some women get real complacent in a relationship after they get you or they just let themselves go and I'm not that attracted anymore. Those are a couple reasons why I've cheated." Bernard answered.

"Damn, I kinda have to agree with Bernard. I cheated on my wife simply like he said the excitement and attraction wasn't there anymore. When we got married she looked amazing. She had her goals in order, she worked her day job, she ate right, she went to the gym four days or sometimes five days a week; I mean she was hot. We had a great sex life and I was absolutely turned on by this woman more than anything. I felt no desire to cheat because I was eager to get back home to my wife. But after like two years had gone by she like changed for whatever reason. She wasn't eating the same and she stopped going to the gym completely. Her shape and looks changed dramatically. She went from being shaped like a coke bottle to looking like a dying Christmas tree. I mean she literally took the figure of someone I would've never dated to begin with. I lost my desire to have sex with her and as time went on it felt like torture. My crave to be attracted to my mate was not appeased and eventually I cheated. I needed that feeling of sexual enjoyment again." Chad answered, very elaborate.

"Now don't get me wrong, I aint making no excuse. Its times I've cheated because I just didn't give a fuck." Bernard added.

"See there, I told you dudes cheat just because." Danielle retorted.

"Aye well he can't speak for all men, I hope you know that." Chad replied.

"Whatever, y'all just don't want to admit it." Danielle said.

"Well...speaking from the side piece's perspective. And yes I've been a side piece; don't judge me. Some of y'all asses is side pieces right now to y'all side pieces." Tamika said as she was interrupted.

"Yo ass is fucking crazy." Tangie cut in, laughing.

"Hey I'm just saying. Long time ago I was seeing a man who was married. We started off cool just kicking it over the phone here and there whenever we could. Eventually we started spending time together in person and it felt good. He told me the reason why he was seeing me is because I simply made him feel good as a man which is something that his wife did not do. I asked him why he didn't just get a divorce and he said because he still loved her and they have children together. He said the relationship had become a disaster full of spite over the years. Arguments took the place of the intimate and sweet conversations they would normally have. He said she was very argumentative, and petty, and there was no respect in their relationship. And we all know where there is no respect there is no good sex, if any, might I add. He said I kissed him the way he wanted to be kissed verses her dry kisses with no feeling. He said I fucked him like I craved him verses her barely having sex with him like it's a boring job she hates to be at. And there you have it why he cheated." Tamika said, sipping her drink.

"Girl BYE! Don't be giving these niggas no excuse for why they cheat. Cheating is in these niggas DNA point blank period." Peaches retorted.

"I aint giving nobody no excuse. You might not like what I'm saying, but it doesn't mean it ain't true. Instead of trying to convince ourselves that all men cheat for no reason, maybe some of us need to look within ourselves and find out if we are pushing our men away with our selfish ways and bad attitudes." Tamika replied.

"Oh so now you being a pick me?" Peaches asked.

"See how you so quick to belittle someone's character and shut down their reasoning just because you don't agree with it? Y'all do the same thing to men and get that nasty look on your face anytime they try to say something positive about their gender or provide any valid points. I ain't saying some men ain't dogs but some of y'all women need to stop automatically shutting men down and consider how they feel and what they have to say. You might be able to recognize how you may be the cause of the problem, or something you can do better and save your relationships. I'm just saying." Tamika replied.

"I wish it was a like button for what the hell you just said. Thank you, thank you, thank you." Kevin said.

"Shut up Kevin." Danielle said, laughing.

"Well can I share something real quick?" Kevin asked.

"Go ahead." Tangie answered.

"And I mean no disrespect to you Peaches or anyone, but if you honestly mean what you say when you say it's in a man's DNA to cheat then why would you get with a man and expect fidelity? Kevin asked.

"What?" Peaches asked, trying to think of her answer.

"Why would you get with a guy expecting fidelity if you honestly feel it's in a man's DNA to cheat?" Kevin respectfully asked.

"Whatever, yall men just ain't shit." Peaches responded, pruning her lips and rolling her eyes.

"Point blank if you want to know what's going on with men then listen to what men have to say instead of recklessly denying what men have to say for the sake of making a point and being right. We tell you how we feel and you can actually learn from us. Other than that you're going to always be clueless about certain things when it comes to us men. However, me personally, I feel that we all know that both men and women cheat; I just think men cheat more. I think us as men were brought up with that pimp playa mentality. All the things we heard our elders say, the gangsta pimp music our elders played around us and what we grew up listening to. Music and TV shows is a major influence especially if it's negative. We don't have honor for our women like we should because we were taught to be against each other. Overall there's a variety of reasons why men or women cheat but we have to be truthful." Kevin expressed.

"Ok, enough about that post. My next post reads; I am a thirty-four year old woman, mother of two. I've been in a beautiful relationship with my boyfriend for almost three years. Normally if we have a disagreement or argument it's something minor and we resolve it peacefully. Just recently we had our most heated argument and have not been able to reconcile. I went to a pool party with some of my girls. When I told my man he didn't have a problem with me going to the pool party; he had a problem with me wearing a two piece bikini. He told me what I had on is equivalent to me wearing a bra and panties in front of strange men. I told him he was insecure and he called me a thirsty attention whore. Am I wrong or is he wrong?" Tangie sipped her liquor and looked around at them for their reaction.

"Oh he's definitely insecure and I can't do no insecure man." Peaches responded.

"Yes, say that shit girl. That shit is a big turn off." Tamika said, shaking her head.

"Yeah, I'm siding with the ladies on this one. I mean what is she supposed to wear to a pool party; a jogging suit?" Bernard asked, sarcastically.

"Yeah, that's some weak as fuck shit right there. I ain't got time for no weak man." Danielle said.

"Let's get a word from another man. Chad, what you think?" Tangie asked.

"Um…I'm just going to say I think it's very insecure of him to have an issue with her wearing a two-piece bikini. I love seeing women in two-piece bikinis. Seeing that ass and those knockers makes my eyes happy." Chad said, being silly but serious.

"Let's get another man in here. Kevin what you think?" Tangie asked.

"Well I think everybody is speaking out of personal gratification and not reality." Kevin answered.

"Wait a minute. What? What the fuck is you talking about?" Bernard asked, face cringed.

"Well since you think I sound crazy let me ask you a logical question. And please keep it real." Kevin said.

"Okay, ask me, I always keep it real." Bernard replied.

Kevin pulled out his phone and went on his Instagram page and pulled up a picture of a woman with a plump fat ass wearing tight booty shorts and a tank top. He showed it to Bernard and asked. "Would you be okay if your woman walked out of your bedroom wearing tight booty shorts and a tank top on all in front of your homeboys?"

"Nigga what? Hell fuck nall, that shit ain't gone happen. My woman would know off RIP I don't play that shit." Bernard replied.

"Why, because she'll be disrespecting you if she did right?" Kevin asked.

"Hell yeah that's disrespectful! I can't believe this is even a question." Bernard said, sarcastically looking around.

Kevin showed it to Danielle and asked. "Danielle, if your man has his friends over watching the Lions game would you walk out the bedroom in front of his boys wearing booty shorts and a halter top?"

"What kind of hoe ass nigga would let his woman wear some booty shorts and a halter top in front of his boys?" Danielle asked, shaking her head.

"Exactly, I agree with you. So y'all actually trying to tell me that it's okay for a woman to wear a two piece bikini in front of a bunch of men BUT she's disrespectful if she walks that ass out in front of her man's boys with booty shorts on, which her ass happens to be more covered up than it is in a bikini? Yall don't see how ass backwards that type of thinking is?" Kevin asked.

"Oh damn, I never thought about it like that. Basically, when she's revealing more of her tits and ass the man is considered insecure if he has a problem with it. However, when she's wearing more clothing and less revealing in her booty shorts the man is considered a hoe ass nigga if he lets his woman wear that and the woman is considered disrespectful." Tamika replied.

"Exactly! But people don't like acknowledging truth and reality. It feels too good to live a false reality." Kevin said.

"So a woman is wrong for wearing a two piece bikini? Boy y'all kill me." Peaches asked.

"In my opinion, yes. However, let me ask you this and be realistic. Would you wear a two-piece bra and panties in front of other men if you're in a relationship?" Kevin asked, downing the rest of his drink.

"What?" Peaches asked.

"You didn't hear the question?" Kevin asked.

"Yeah I heard you. I mean of course I wouldn't wear a bra and panties in front of another man if I'm in a relationship." Peaches replied with a stank look on her face, trying to avoid the logic.

"Then how is it disrespectful if a woman in a relationship wears a two piece bra and panties in front of men other than her mate but it's not disrespectful to wear a two piece bikini in front of other men?" Kevin asked very reasonably.

"It's different, one is a bikini and the other is underwear, duh." Peaches said, slightly irritated.

"So you're trying to tell me that it's the title of the garment that determines if it's disrespectful?" Kevin asked.

"What? One is a bikini and the other is underwear." Peaches replied.

"It's not the name, not the style, nor the material the garment is made of that makes it disrespectful. It's the certain parts of the body that is revealed that makes it disrespectful." Kevin intelligently expressed.

"Yeah but if a setting like the beach calls for it then how is it disrespectful?" Bernard asked.

"Disrespect is disrespect no matter what setting it is. What if your mate went to a nude beach and stripped naked in front of everybody should you say I guess there's nothing wrong with it since the setting called for them to be nude?" Chad asked.

By this time people's drinks had kicked in and the conversation got a bit more insidious and sarcastic.

"You know what? Fuck this shit; I don't give a fuck what y'all say. Niggas gone be dogs and be thirsty and hound us women and get jealous because women got choices. Women fuck who they want to fuck and men fuck who they can." Danielle said.

"And Men marry who we want to marry and Women marry who they can." Chad retorted.

"Oh shit." Tamika said, feeling the tension.

Danielle frowned her face at his ass and brushed Chad off and he nonchalantly ignored her like she wasn't shit. At this point Tangie decided to exit from the conversation and take Peaches with her. "Look y'all getting to deep for me right now. I'm showing this ass regardless to who like it or don't like it. Now if yall will excuse me I needs me another drink."

Peaches and Tangie headed over to the drink table while talking shit about how that conversation got deep and went left. Tangie tapped Peaches quickly on the arm and told her to look to her far right at the three handsome gentlemen. They were standing there talking to two ladies, Kandis and Yolanda.

"They better be careful, they talking to two of the biggest hoes in the company." Peaches said, pouring her a drink.

"That bitch Kandis don't like me. She always trying to one up somebody any time no matter what the conversation is." Tangie said, pouring her a drink as well.

"Trust me, Yolanda the same muthafuckin way. You can be standing there telling somebody how blessed you was to make it out of a life-threatening situation. I guarantee that bitch will immediately conjure up a story just to out-bless your story and shit." Peaches replied.

"You are a damn fool." Tangie said, laughing at what Peaches said.

"Look fuck them skank ass hoes." Peaches said, pulling out her Galaxy Note 9 cellphone and turning her selfie mode on.

"Yes, fuck em." Tangie replied, putting her arm around Peaches waist and looking up at the camera.

"Ok smile." Peaches said as she used her S-Pen to snap several pictures of themselves.

"Take one more." Tangie said as they made funny faces.

"I'm about to post these sexy fine ass pics onto Facebook and Instagram." Peaches said, looking at her social media feed.

"Make sure you tag me in those pics." Tangie said sipping her drink.

"Girl I know what to do; you ain't gotta tell me that." Peaches said, posting their pics.

"Oooohhh girl look at these two sexy, chocolate, bearded, fine ass men over there looking all delicious and shit." Tangie said, licking her lips.

Peaches looked up "Damn you ain't lying."

"I would ride the fuck out of his sexy face and saturate his beard with this all-natural beard butter." Tangie said.

"What the fuck is wrong with these niggas?" Peaches asked, face frowned up looking at her phone.

"What? What happen?" Tangie looked over at Peaches, excited to hear some bullshit.

"These niggas always up in my inbox with this bullshit. Sending me dick pic after dick pic, asking for my number and sending me theirs. Bad thing about it is half these niggas got a whole wife or woman at home." Peaches stressed with an attitude.

"Girl these niggas stay in my inbox with that bullshit too." Tangie added, shaking her head.

"It aint even been five minutes since I posted those pics, and niggaz is hitting my inbox up already." Peaches replied.

"Girl!" Tangie replied, feeling what peaches just said.

"And this one dude he in my inbox all the fucking time with his lame ass. I ignore his ass every single time and he keep sending me his whack ass dick pics." Peaches said.

"Hey do like I do and put they ass on blast on a post." Tangie said.

"Yep, if it happens again that's exactly what I'm doing." Peaches replied.

"Hey I forgot to tell you that yo boo looking for you with his fine ass." Tangie said.

"My boo? What you talking about?" Peaches sipped her drink.

"Yo boo DeYonte." Tangie answered.

"Girl bye, I'm about to go to my cubical. I'll be right back." Peaches said.

"Okay and I'm about to sachet my way pass them sexy bearded men and get their attention. Might find my husband tonight." Tangie said hilarious and walked off.

Peaches headed to her cubical to get something out of her purse that she had locked in her desk drawer. She had a really good buzz going on and thought to herself ***Damn it's dark back here.*** She flipped the light switch on as she walked down the aisle way and said ***And let there be light.*** She stepped in her cubical and scratched her head with a puzzled look. She started feeling in her pockets and looking around curiously. ***Aw fuck, don't tell me I left them in my purse…*** She grabbed the drawer handle and tugged on it just to find out it was locked. ***Damn*** she looked over on her desk to see if she had left her keys there. She lifted the letter tray to see if she hid them under there but saw nothing but a few pieces of paper. She looked over to see if they were hanging on the hooks she had mounted on her wall but they weren't there either. ***Damn what the hell did I do with my keys.***

"Hey." DeYonte said, standing behind her.

He startled the shit out of Peaches as she immediately turned around! "Oh my God don't do that shit. Sneaking up on folks scaring the shit out of people like that."

"My bad beautiful. Can I help you find whatever it is that you're looking for?" DeYonte asked, standing close and looking at her like a delicious hot chocolate pie.

Peaches looked at his lips and replied. "DeYonte, um go stand yo ass over there. I'm looking for my keys, help me look by looking from over there."

DeYonte was five-ten and a half, bald headed and nicely chiseled. He had a very neat goatee, tatted arms and smelled like Savage cologne.

"Damn, you are so damn sexy and beautiful to me. You should just let me treat you out sometime like old times." DeYonte slowly looked her up and down and back at her eyes.

"DeYonte…I'm going through something right now. Besides I need you to help me find my keys right now." Peaches said as she turned around and glanced behind her paper shredder.

DeYonte stepped over to the garbage can and tried to glance through it. "I think I heard somebody say someone found some keys up front.

Peaches happened to look to her left and notice her coworker Randy just standing there looking.

"What the…why are you just standing there watching me like that?" Peaches paused and asked.

Randy stuttered for a second, holding her keys up. "Um someone told me these may be yours."

"Yes those are mine. Who had them?" Peaches asked as she walked over and grabbed them from him.

"I forget the lady name, but she handed them to me to give to you." Randy answered.

"Okay well thank you." Peaches said, glancing at him awkwardly.

"Oh yeah, no problem. You're welcome. Sorry to disturb you." Randy replied, nodding his head at Peaches and giving a snide glance at DeYonte as he walked away.

DeYonte waited till Randy got far enough away and continued conversing with Peaches.

"Damn that nigga is strange, I'm telling you his elevator don't go all the way to the top. You see how he looked at me?" DeYonte asked.

"Yeah he's a bit on the weird side, he needs help bad." Peaches replied, opening her drawer and grabbing her purse.

"So back to where we were." DeYonte said, easing up close to her again.

Peaches turned around again and leaned against her desk. "Um where the hell were we? Last time I checked you was supposed to be over there." Replying sarcastically, pointing on the other side of the cubical.

Out of the blue they could hear someone approaching. "Aye DeYonte, where yo ass at?" Kandis asked.

Peaches looked at DeYonte "Oh shit you better get yo hoes."

"What? Yeah right, I don't have no hoes." DeYonte replied, incredulous facial expression.

Kandis stopped at Peaches cubical when she saw DeYonte standing there talking to Peaches. She gave him a slight evil ass look.

"Oh I didn't mean to disturb yall; hopefully I didn't interrupt nothing." Kandis said, slight sarcasm.

"Nope." Peaches replied.

"Wsup Kandis?" DeYonte asked, thinking she was about to say some stupid shit.

"Nothing Mr. Inbox King. Keep doing you." Kandis replied.

"I'm lost." DeYonte replied, shaking his head.

"Oh Peaches, I found your keys. I gave them to that weird boy to give to you." Kandis said, very subtle attitude.

"Oh...okay...thank you." Peaches replied, thinking to herself why the fuck would you give my keys to him out of all people.

"Welp I aint gone hold yall up." Kandis replied sarcastically and walked off.

"Why yall niggaz don't know how to keep yall hoes in check?" Peaches asked, shaking her head.

"I told you I aint got no hoes. I don't know what you talking about." DeYonte replied.

"Well yall got something going on. You all up in her inbox so you must be saying something that got her stalking you around the workplace and giving me dirty looks." Peaches replied, slipping out from in front of him.

"Why do yall women always feed off the first thing a woman say as if it's automatically the truth and thinking she's some type of victim?" DeYonte asked.

"I mean she feel that way about something you said to her. I wouldn't think she would just be saying it if you wasn't in her inbox saying something to her." Peaches answered, looking at him sideways.

"And that's exactly what I'm talking about right there. Yall are just in total disbelief that a man can just be in a woman's inbox just having a cool conversation with no sexual intent to it." DeYonte said.

"So you trying to have cool conversation but you not trying to fuck her? What's the purpose of having a conversation with her if you're not trying to advance at some point? Women already know what yall men are about. Yall want two things, sex and more sex." Peaches sarcasm is irritating.

"So a man just can't have a conversation with a woman without trying to have sex with her? You trying to tell me that conversation is irrelevant if I'm not trying to pursue a relationship and have sex with her?" DeYonte asked.

"Okay, so what you in her inbox for? I want to hear this shit." Peaches looked at him.

"The same reason yall women be in a man's inbox; just trying to vibe with a person and feel them out; see where their head at and perhaps learn something from them." DeYonte answered.

"Bullshit." Peaches retorted.

"So when you in a man's inbox are you trying to fuck him?" DeYonte asked.

"Nope." Peaches just looked at him.

"Now who's full of shit?" DeYonte asked.

"I aint full of shit; yall niggaz be full of shit. Yall not like us women." Peaches replied.

"Not only are you full of shit but you're very sexist and irrational." DeYonte said, surprised at her comments.

"Sexist? Irrational? Who?" Peaches asked.

"The owl, that's who." DeYonte sarcastically replied.

"Me? No the hell I'm not. Yall men just don't like hearing about yall selves." Peaches grabbed her purse and zipped it closed.

"No, we get tired of women pretending they don't do shit wrong. Yall get amnesia when it comes down to what yall do wrong but yall excellent at trying to point out what a man do. Just be real like yall ask us men to be real." DeYonte replied.

"Whatever." Peaches responded.

"And for the record; when a man finds himself in multiple women's inboxes this is how it happens in many cases. A man will notice an attractive woman and have a cool conversation with her. If the vibe is good he'll start to dig her a bit more and engage in more conversations with her. At that point they may exchange numbers; hell they may even exchange nude pics. However at some point of getting to know her he ultimately notices something that's a serious red flag and realizes she is not his type of chic he would really like to date. At that point he'll slowly back away and just keep it on a friend level; no harm is done. Doesn't mean he can't continue talking to her. The problem comes in when there's a sense of entitlement and obligation just because you had a few conversations with someone. Some folks will talk to you like you're in a committed relationship and be questioning you and checking you." DeYonte preached.

"I mean, you can't fault a woman for developing expectations and wanting more after having good conversation with someone especially if she likes him." Peaches replied.

"Yeah but you also just can't assume someone is trying to pursue a relationship with you or have sex with you just based off of a general conversation either." DeYonte stressed.

"Yall men will never understand. All yall know is cheat, cheat and more cheat." Peaches said.

"Why do you have to respond irrationally instead of gaining an understanding with me?" DeYonte asked.

"Like I said, yall just cheat, cheat, cheat. Yall men should learn from us." Peaches replied.

"And for the record… just because SOME women don't cheat doesn't mean their good women or relationship material. They can just be loyal women with fuck ass shitty personalities. And by the way I've already been informed by a couple female therapist and friends that most women cheat. Yall just want to pretend that yall don't to not sound hypocritical."

IDOL TIME IS A DEVIL'S PLAYGROUND

Friday – September 13, 2019 – 8:15pm – Liquor store.

"Let me get a fifth and a pint of Hennessy please." Antonio requested, putting his cherry Pepsi and small bag of ice on the counter.

The clerk returned with the bottles, rung him up and bagged everything. "That'll be sixty-sixty-two please."

"Oh and let me get one of your small plastic cups." Antonio requested, watching the clerk put the cup in the bag.

Antonio paid for everything, thanked the clerk and left. He got in the car, cracked open the pint and poured himself a cup. He took a sip, put the fifth in the back seat and pulled off. He was in a chill mode, listening to smooth music and pondering his situation with Peaches. Hennessey and ice cubes swirled in Antonio's plastic cup as he cruised through the city streets. He imagined if she was out fucking with another dude and just shook his head. However, he had no way of actually knowing what she was doing at the time and he damn sure wasn't about to call her. He turned down Shawn's street and could see a couple people on his front porch. It was Shawn's fine ass sister Bridgette and one of her girls sitting on the steps talking. Bridgette smiled and tapped her girl on the leg as Antonio pulled up and parked. He grabbed the bag with the Henny off the back seat and got out.

"Well, well, well look at what the wind blew in." Bridgette said, getting up to hug him as he approached the porch.

"Hey sweetie, how you doing?" Antonio asked, smiling.

"I'm feeling good now; my baby daddy here." Bridgette answered, looking at him up and down.

"Aw shit." Antonio replied, giving her a hug.

"When you gone let me hit that?" Bridgette asked, being silly but for real.

"Damn only if thangs were different." Antonio replied, smirking and shaking his head.

"You worried about my brother Shawn? Fuck him; he don't control who I fuck with." Bridgette said.

"I ain't worried about that." Antonio replied.

"Oh I forgot you got a woman don't you?" Bridgette asked, looking at him sideways.

"Yeah…" Antonio said, sounding reluctant.

"You didn't sound too confident when you just said that." Bridgette replied.

"Yeah…we sort of split apart at the moment." Antonio said, reluctant to put his business out there.

"So yall separated?" Bridgette asked.

"Yeah pretty much." Antonio answered.

"And you still loyal? Damn you must be a unicorn because I know I look good; don't no man turn me down. I'm just being honest." Bridgette said, stunned.

"Right." Denise added, shocked as well.

"As attractive as you are, of course they don't." Antonio replied.

"Let me ask you something." Bridgette said.

"Shoot it." Antonio replied, remotely locking his car.

"Why do men cheat?" Bridgette asked.

"Wow that's a very broad question because there are various reasons men cheat and no two men think exactly the same. So I can't give you a definite answer but I will tell you this. I honestly believe part of the reason is we were bred to be this way especially us black men in particular." Antonio said.

"Now this is interesting, I wasn't expecting to hear that." Denise retorted.

"I mean look at the type of music we've listened to as children. It's easy to learn in rhythm and jingles because they subconsciously stick with you forever. It doesn't matter if its nursery rhymes or Gangsta lyrics it always sticks with you. These rappers get paid millions of dollars and are immortalized for getting fast money, fast cars, countless women and reckless sex. It's a negative influence our men and women glorify. Why wouldn't our young boys be inspired to have this same mentality?

"You definitely have a point." Denise said.

"Then you got some people who cheat just because they're bored. Some people cheat because their desires are neglected. Some men cheat simply because they feel it's a man's rite of passage. Not to mention we are not taught to love like our girls get taught to love. Our boys are taught to be hard by their mothers and fathers. He gets punched in the chest by his mother or father if he displays any type of feelings or sensitivity. So he grows up to be hard and unable to properly embrace true love and just chases pussy." Antonio stated.

"Finally we get a few straight up answers from a man." Bridgette.

"Being that I kept it real with you let me ask you something and I want you to keep it real with me. Why do women cheat?" Antonio asked.

"Well women cheat for a few reasons. One we cheat if we're not sexually satisfied. Number two we cheat if we're being neglected and we not getting any quality time. And I know I'm breaking the girl code with this one, but number three we cheat because we feel like fuckin with another nigga point blank. He might be breaking a bitch off them coins and that dick. I can go on but that's enough female game for you and shit. I cant give you all our secrets." Bridgette confided.

"Thank you for that baby." Antonio replied.

"So have you ever cheated on the woman you were just currently with?" Bridgette asked.

"No I haven't." Antonio answered.

"Really, why not?" Denise asked.

"Because I valued her." Antonio answered.

"Valued?... Damn…Value…" Bridgette pondered, soaking in what he said.

"Remember this; we take pride in, and protect that which we have honor for and find value in. The right woman will retain the loyalty of a good man, trust me." Antonio replied.

"If you don't mind me asking; what made her valuable to you?" Brigette asked.

"Just who she was overall. We were compatible mentally, spiritually and I was absolutely attracted to her physically; she was everything that I lust for in a woman. She wasn't selfish; she was there for me financially when I never asked or expected her to be. She was the total package for me. That's when she won my mind and devotion and I let the rest of the women in my life go." Antonio said.

"Mmm you so intelligent." Bridgette said.

"Thank you sweetie. Well hey, let me get on in here with the fellas before they start blowing my phone up." Antonio replied, heading for the side door.

"Okay." Bridgette replied.

"Nice talking to you and thank you for the information." Denise said, lowkey wanting a piece of him too.

"Nice talking with yall as well." Antonio replied.

"Tell your girl she is lucky." Bridgette stated.

"Okay I will baby." Antonio said, chuckling.

"And if yall don't get back together you come get this value I got for you." Bridgette said, smirking.

"Yeah okay Bridgette, I hear you." Antonio said, trying to refrain from the thought that he could fuck Bridgette if he pursued it.

Antonio knocked on the side door; he could hear them all the way from outside; talking loud as fuck and laughing. He looked behind him after hearing the heavy breathing of the neighbor's dog in the backyard brushing up against the fence. It was always funny how this big fierce looking black dog never barked; he just looked at you with his tongue hanging out the side of his mouth and breathing fast. He held the bag up at the dog playfully teasing him ***You want some of this boy? Nope, sorry dogs can't have none of this.*** The dog barked because he wanted what was in that bag; preferably doggy treats. Antonio shook his head ***Yo ass probably would drink this shit.*** He turned around to knock on the door once again but that's when the door opened. It was Shawn's woman, a thick sista with a fat ass.

"Hey Antonio, come on in." Marlo said, greeting him with a friendly hug as he stepped inside.

"Hey Marlo, how are you?" Antonio asked.

"I'm okay; they all downstairs." Marlo said.

"Ok, thank you, Sis." Antonio said, as he made his way downstairs to holla at the fellas.

Halfway down the staircase he's greeted with marijuana smoke, loud talk and a garbage pail of empty red liquor cups. Before he even got down the stairs all the way somebody was already talking shit.

"Don't tell me you came over to this muthafucka empty handed nigga? Where the drank at?" Shawn asked playfully, looking up at Antonio.

Shawn was a six foot-two, two-hundred-and-sixty-pound baby-faced bully. He was goofy, always had jokes, but was also down for the slime life.

"Nigga, do I ever come empty handed?" Antonio asked, showing his bag in his hand.

"Wdup doh, nigga?" Tim stood up, giving Antonio dap.

"What's good my nigga?" Antonio replied.

Tim was definitely a hood nigga and was Shawn's right hand man. Average height, dark skinned, big bucket Detroit baseball cap and hoodie. Antonio turned to his cousin Desmond who was coming to show his love.

"Playboy, wdup doh." Desmond said, giving him dap as well.

"Yo, what it do, what it do Cuz?" Antonio replied.

"What's good homie?" Shawn asked.

"Shit, chillin, chillin." Antonio replied, taking the fifth of Hennessy out of the bag and sitting it on the card table.

"Shit I'm surprised this nigga out the house. Ever since your girl moved in you been on house arrest and shit." Shawn said.

"Sheeeiiiddd that nigga a free agent now; that's why his ass is out the muthafuckin house." Desmond replied, sipping his drink.

"What? You and your girl broke up?" Shawn asked, animated.

"Naw it aint like that, we just taking a break." Antonio replied, not really wanting his relationship matters to be the topic of discussion.

"Aw shit nigga, you know what a break mean? That's free agency and you free to test the market. Somebody might be bang banging that ass right now." Shawn joked, taking a puff of the weed.

"Nigga smoke that shit and shut the fuck up." Antonio replied, taking off his jacket and sitting down.

"Aw shit him sensitive about his baby." Shawn replied.

"Shawn, he gone kick yo ass…after he find out you right!" Tim said, laughing.

"Oh yall niggas real funny today huh?" Antonio said, pouring him a drink.

"Naw we just fucking with you my nigga. BUT we are going to get yo mind off all of that bullshit tonight though. You aint gone be thinking about no relationship shit I guarantee, trust me." Shawn said, passing the weed to Tim.

"Man, what the fuck yall talking about?" Antonio asked, sipping his liquor.

"Don't worry about what the fuck we talking about. Yo ass is a free agent so you coming with us, point blank." Tim replied.

“Yup, it’s too late, it’s already a done deal. Nigga you rolling with Rush tonight bro, so relax.” Shawn said.

“Nothing but big asses and titties everywhere; I can’t wait!” Tim said with the stank face acting like he squeezing a fat ass with both of his hands.

“Aw shit I already know what the fuck yall talking about.” Antonio replied, laughing.

“No retreat, no surrender now my nigga.” Shawn said, jokingly.

“Nigga, you aint afraid to go to the strip club right?" Desmond asked, looking at Antonio while flipping through a magazine he grabbed off the top of a small stand.

“Aye nigga, I’m all good. Yeah I’m going, aint nothing wrong with sight-seeing.” Antonio answered.

“Lies. I should give yo ass five dollars for lying so damn fast.” Tim said, laughing.

“Take advantage of it while you can. You know yo girl aint gone let you go to no strip club if yall get back together.” Shawn said.

“Nigga, I’m sure yo woman aint just willing to let you go to the strip club.” Antonio said, looking at Shawn.

“Nigga shit, my woman takes ME to the muthafuckin strip club so she don’t give a fuck if I go with my niggas. And the reason why she don’t give a fuck is because she know Ima break her off this dick when I get back home so she good with it.” Shawn replied.

“What the fuck?” Desmond abruptly said, pointing in the magazine.

“What? Must be some ass.” Tim asked, walking over to take a look.

“Let me see.” Antonio said, easing over to look.

“Damn, she fine than a muthafucka!” Tim said, gazing at the page.

"Oh yeah, well look at this page my nigga." Desmond said as he flipped the page to the previous page.

"Damn, that's how she really looks?" Antonio asked.

"Yes sir." Desmond nodded his head dramatically.

"Damnnnnnnn.... What level of sorcery her make up artist use to turn her ugly ass into this?" Antonio asked.

"Nigga you know you'll hit that without the makeup." Tim said.

"You crazy as a muthafucka if you think that bullshit. It ain't enough Hennessy and cocaine combined to make me do no shit like that." Antonio replied.

"Aye man, while yall niggaz over there fantasizing about yall future wife we need to be getting ready to go see some of them big booty hoes up on them poles." Shawn said, puffing the weed.

"Aye nigga I'm ready." Desmond replied.

"Nigga, I been ready." Tim said, turning his cup up and downed the rest of his drink.

"And dig this, we hitting Chocolate City tonight and Crazyhorse tomorrow." Shawn said.

"Nigga I'm ready!" Tim replied, amped rubbing his hands together.

"Man it's gone be so much ass in that muthafucka tomorrow! All the big booty all-stars gone be in that bitch, I'm telling you!" Shawn replied.

"They must be having a stripper contest going on up in that bitch." Desmond said.

"You know what else gone be up in there tomorrow? That Moolah...all the ballers gone be there." Tim said.

"Oh yes nigga, you know what time it is. Time to get them bread sticks; run me that paper nigga!" Shawn replied, looking at Tim.

Fuck Boy

A front door unlocks and a young lady steps inside the house shutting the door behind her. She kicks her shoes off, sets them in the corner neatly and heads to her bedroom in the back. As she passes through the dining room, she noticed her brother's laptop laying on the table. What caught her attention was a picture of one of her homegirls on the screen. She leaned forward with an incredulous look on her face thinking ***What the fuck is this nigga doing?*** By that time, he was coming down the stairs and noticed her looking at his computer.

"Damn bro, why you all in my shit?" Dough-Boy asked her.

"First of all, I'm not your bro; I'm your sister. Secondly, aint nobody all in your shit trying to see shit. I just happened to see my girl picture on your computer screen which by the way is very creepy." Lisa answered, looking at him weird.

"It wouldn't be creepy if you wasn't all in my business." Dough-Boy said, immediately shutting his laptop.

"I'm not trying to be in your business but I do get tired of my friends and coworkers telling me how you sending them friend request, random strange messages and pictures of your nasty little penis." Lisa replied.

"I can message who the hell I want to message; if they don't like it fuck them hoes." Dough-Boy said.

"Why do you have to be a disrespectful nigga? The way you think is ignorant like a little boy." Lisa stated.

"Look fuck you and them hoes; yall don't control what the fuck I do." Dough-Boy said, slight frown on his face.

"And the ignorant shit you be posting and saying about black women on your page and in these groups is lame shit. You act like you hate black women." Lisa said.

"Yall black women act like yall perfect and don't do shit wrong and yall avoid accountability. Yall make posts about black men and dog us out daily and got the nerve to complain when we talk about yall ass back. Yes we get tired of hearing and reading that shit and this is why I say what I say about yall ass." Dough-Boy replied, eloquently.

"This is my problem with ignorant fools like you. I'm a black woman and I know black women trash black men on social media and I don't support that shit. Yet dudes like you tend to avoid the fact that all black women ain't out here wronging black men. I'm a black woman and I'm your sister and you know for a fact I don't do that shit. Your mother is a black woman WHOM you are currently living with basically rent free. Aint NO BODY got your back more than her. You need to think about that shit and check yourself the next time you feel the urge to generalize black women period." Lisa retorted emphatically.

"Aye you do know you're living here with momma too, right?" Dough-Boy said sarcastically.

"Well at least I haven't been here as long as you and I have an exit plan. You on the other hand are a grown ass man living here not making any effort to get your own place. You're online every single day stalking and harassing women. You do know that's fuck boy shit right?" Lisa asked.

"Lisa mind your muthafuckin business and stay the hell out of mine." Dough-Boy replied, grabbing his laptop and heading to his room.

"You should change your social media name from Dough-Boy to Fuck Boy." Lisa said and walked to her room.

Dough-Boy shook his head and walked in his room. ***Stupid little nosey ass; can't get no privacy around this bitch.*** The light from the computer screen shinned on his face as he sat on the bed in his dark room scrolling on his Facebook page. He always kept his door shut and locked so his mother or his sister wouldn't just walk in unexpectedly. He was weird as fuck and always posting dumb shit on his page and in private groups he'd joined. His awkward look and disposition made women look at him like a creep and he despised it. He never in his life developed good social skills with the ladies. However, he developed a hidden hate and lack of respect for women because they dissed him and made fun of him growing up. He sipped his juice and shook his head ***damn this bitch right here thick as fuck and got a fat ass.*** He was in desperate need of a hair cut, his beard was unshaved and his breath stunk like rat ass. He clicked on her page and liked several pictures of hers. He backed out and clicked on her friends list and continued scrolling. He noticed this particular chic he really found attractive. ***Got damn this bitch fine!*** He clicked on her pic and realized he had already sent her a friend request. It was still pending but it showed he was following her. He clicked on her photos and got excited sucking his teeth and grabbing his dick! ***Oh fuck! Look at this hoe's dsl's. Damn I'll bust all on her mouth! Muthafuckin Mz. Peaches with yo sexy ass.*** He noticed that her status said she was in a relationship with Antonio James. ***What kinda nigga got two first names as***

one whole name and shit? He clicked on to his page and sent him a friend request. He retracted the friend request and decided to just follow him. He looked through his photos for a moment and backed off of his page. He got back on to Peaches page and decided to send her a inbox.

11:54pm

Dough Boy – Wsup baby, you looking thick and sexy as fuck. Can I get to know you? Call me 313 990-3499

11:56pm

Dough Boy – You should let a nigga invite you ova to da crib. We need to get to know each other.

11:57pm

Dough Boy – I bet you laying in yo bed looking sexy af. I bet yo juicy booty smell good and taste good. If I was yo man I'll be eaten yo ass every night.

12:01am

Dough Boy – Damn you too good to talk back to a nigga? You prolly the stuck up type.

12:06am

Dough Boy – My bad for saying that. Good night

Dough Boy clicked on to a couple of her pictures and saved them to his phone. He started touching himself and fondling his dick. He clicked on his selfie camera and lied back on his bed. He imagined her sucking his dick until he got hard and took a picture of it. At that point he took it upon himself to bless her inbox with his dick pic.

He opened up his picture gallery on his phone, pulled up her picture and started intensely jacking off.

JUST A FRIENDLY STROLL

Saturday - September 14th 2019 - 4:37pm - Woodward Ave. The sound of Peaches high heels clicked across the concrete as she and DeYonte strolled up the remodeled streets of Downtown Detroit Michigan. Various restaurants and boutiques adorned the Ave and people were everywhere window shopping and patronizing. The smell of grilled steak and chicken cooked to perfection catches the attention as you walk pass. It made your mouth water for some of that delicious smelling food even if you weren't hungry. The sound of the Q-Line dinged as the trolley cruised by. Peaches couldn't believe she was out walking with DeYonte after vowing to Antonio she was just going to do her. DeYonte looked up as the People Mover passed by just above.

"Damn, I don't think I've ridden the people mover since I was a kid." DeYonte said.

Peaches looked up at it and smiled. "Yeah it's been a minute since I've been on it to. Matter fact the last time I've been on it I was just a little girl and my father would take me on it, he'd call it the L – Train in the sky. After he passed away I haven't been on it since."

"Hmmm really? The L-Train in the sky; I like that." DeYonte replied, thinking.

"Yeah…that's what my daddy would call it. I miss my Daddy taking me on there." Peaches reminisced.

"Hey…how's about you and I relive our childhood moments right now and take a trip around downtown?" DeYonte asked.

"On the L-Train in the sky, really?" Peaches asked, cheesing.

"Yes, really. There's the boarding station right over there." DeYonte answered.

"Okay, I'd love to." Peaches said with excited eyes.

They looked both ways and crossed the busy street of Woodward headed over to the people mover boarding station.

"Damn downtown is lit right now!" Peaches said, looking over at Hart Plaza.

"Yeah, I forget what festival is going on right now, but whatever it is it's on jam." DeYonte said.

"If I'm correct it's the Fall Beer Tasting Boat Cruise going on right now." Peaches said.

"Oh okay." DeYonte replied.

They made it to the People Mover boarding station. DeYonte opened the door ***Ladies first.*** DeYonte paid the toll for them to proceed going up stairs to board. Peaches walked up the stairs in front of him; he wanted to sniff and kiss her bare ass with each step. They hurried up because they could hear the next train pulling around. Peaches smiled with excitement as it was slowing down in front of her. They got on board and held onto the rails as the People Mover took off again.

"God, I haven't been on this in so long." Peaches said, sitting down and gazing at the view of downtown from above outside the window.

"It's beautiful aint it?" DeYonte said, sitting down and looking out the window as well.

"Downtown is starting to truly come together and is really fun to be a part of." Peaches smiled, looking down at all of the people and scenery.

"Yes, it's very nice; all of the restaurants and boutiques, the festivals etc. It's beautiful…like you." DeYonte said.

Peaches smiled and looked over at DeYonte and replied. "Thank you."

He looked at her and smiled and then he walked over and eased down beside her. He placed his hand gently over her hand. Her heart throbbed a little even though she maintained her composer. She had a feeling where this attraction might be headed and exhaled.

"Look…Peaches…I think you're very beautiful and I like you… I like you a lot. You know I've been liking you for a while, and what happened between us was mind blowing. I've been thinking of you every day since." DeYonte said.

"DeYonte…that should've never happened." Peaches said, thinking of Antonio.

"Dang, why you say it like that?" DeYonte asked, feeling empty inside.

"I'm not saying it as a diss to you. I'm saying my emotions was conflicting with my mind because I still love someone else. Besides sexual energy between two people will disable your conscious and regrets until after the fun is over. Then your regrets will come to haunt you with overwhelming guilt." Peaches replied, looking over at him.

DeYonte just nodded his head with a straight face and continued looking out the window.

"Look, I'm sorry if I hurt you. I didn't mean to…" Peaches said, grabbing her phone to check it after it vibrated.

"No I'm cool; I can't get mad if someone doesn't like me." DeYonte said.

"It's not like that; like I said I got something going on in my life right now, but at least I know you checking for me." Peaches replied.

"And speaking of checking for somebody. How come your girl call herself checking me about you?" DeYonte asked.

"My girl? My girl who?" Peaches asked with a serious incredulous look on her face.

"Kandis." DeYonte answered.

"Kandis? That bitch better get a life and stay the fuck out of mine if she know what's good for her crazy ass." Peaches replied.

"Hell yeah she crazy crazy, talking about if I keep on its going to be a problem." DeYonte said, shaking his head.

"Keep on doing what?? Aye, all I know is you better get that forty dollar hoe before I do or she gone really have some problems. Because if she come up in my face talking that dumb shit I promise you Ima drag that ass from Woodward Avenue to the Canadian border." Peaches replied, grabbing her phone because it vibrated.

"Damn." DeYonte replied.

A nasty scowl appeared on Peaches face as she stared at her phone. "What the hell is wrong with these, niggas?" Peaches asked, shaking her head.

DeYonte recognized that her demeanor had changed.

"You alright?" DeYonte asked.

"Yeah… I'm alright…" Peaches answered.

"Um…that didn't sound to convincing." DeYonte said.

"These dudes are so fuckin disrespectful. This dude named Dough Boy keeps sending me dick pics and harassing messages in my inbox and I'm sick of it." Peaches said, irritated.

"Let me see this dude; click on his profile." DeYonte said.

Peaches clicked on his profile and handed the phone to DeYonte. "Here you go. He sent me this shit last night."

DeYonte had an incredulous look on his face as he glanced over the messages and looked at the guys picture. "Wait a minute; What the fuck?" DeYonte asked.

"What?..." Peaches asked.

"This that nigga Randy from our job." DeYonte replied.

"What the fuck?! Let me see that." Peaches said, reaching for her phone.

"Trust me its him." Deyonte said.

Peaches sneered as she looked at this dude picture. "How can you tell? The picture looks blurry."

"His ass sent me a friend request a while back. I didn't recognize his ass at first because of this stupid profile pic he has up. Then his other pictures he has on here are random dumb shit. Then I typed his name in the search box and found out he had another page with all of his pictures on it and I found out it was Randy. Let me show you his other profile with this very same photo and more." DeYonte pulled out his phone and pulled up Randy's other profile.

Peaches inquisitively grabbed his phone and looked. She swiped through a few of his pictures and it was definitely Randy. "I can't believe this pathetic stalking nigga has been the one sending me this shit. Oh my God let me pull him up on my phone right now."

"Oh shit, this nigga done got you started." DeYonte said.

"Oh he got me started alright; he don't have a clue. He ain't dealt with nobody like me before I bet you." Peaches said, thumbs were moving like a sewing machine.

"What you over there doing?" DeYonte asked.

"I just pulled up his other page and screen shot his pics. I'm going to copy and paste them with these sick dic pics and messages he keeps sending me and post them on my page and in the group he followed me in." Peaches said.

"Oh damn, shits about to get real." DeYonte said, being funny.

"Oh it's about to get real alright, it's about to get really real." Peaches said as she made the post.

CrazyHorse

Saturday night – September 14th, 2019 - 9:57pm… CrazyHorse strip club, one of the more classier Gentlemen's clubs in Detroit. The song "Booty" by Blac Youngster was beating through the speakers as they all paid to get in and entered. The blue colored walls, light blue ceiling lights and smoke from the stage set the ambience. There was elongated 30 foot in length stage in the center of the room. There was a pole on each end of the stage with a sexy stripper on each one. They were giving one hell of a show captivating the fuck out of the crowd. A recap of one of the NBA 2019 season opening games was playing on the flat screens; L.A Lakers versus L.A Clippers. Lebron James and Anthony Davis verses Kawhi Leonard and Paul George were showcasing an epic battle for western conference supremacy. The fellas had paid for a booth up along the wall right in front of the stairs where the strippers step down off the stage. The atmosphere and energy was exhilarating as they walked through. He hugged one of the strippers that he knew who was standing there talking to two other strippers. He said something in her ear, smacked her on the ass and she smiled as they proceeded walking pass. A couple young drug dealers with big bucket baseball caps and sagging jeans were making it rain for the babes up on the pole. Fives's, ten's and twenty-dollar bills wafted from the ceiling down onto the stage and the floor. The fellas paid that no mind as they could feel all eyes were on them as they moved through the people approaching their booth.

A gorgeous waitress with long hair and slanted eyes came over to their table and asked them if she could get them something to drink. They sat down and ordered food, and a couple bottles; Rosay and Hennessey was the drink of choice. A dude from the booth next to them got up and walked towards their table. Antonio noticed him as he was approaching and realized it was his cousin, Excel.

"Wdup doh, cuz?" Antonio got up and shook hands with him.

"What's good, bro?" Excel asked.

"Slow motion, just out here hanging with the fellas. Aye, you remember my niggas Shawn, and Tim?" Antonio asked as he looked to Shawn and Tim.

Shawn stood up, looking at Excel and asked "Wdup doh, cuz? Yeah, I remember my dude. What's good?" Shawn asked as he shook his hand.

"Wdup bro?" Excel asked.

"That's a dog ass chain you wearing; that bitch a beast." Shawn said, admiring Excels necklace.

"Thanks my nigga." Excel replied.

"Wuz good my nigga?" Timmy asked as he shook his hand.

Desmond stood up and asked "Wdup muthafucka?!"

"Wdup cousin?" Excel asked as they shook hands and hugged.

"Who you here with?" Desmond asked.

"Just some of my dogs. Wanted to get out and see some ass and tits for a moment." Desmond answered.

By that time the DJ asked for the next dancer to come to the stage. ***Majesty, you up next***. Majesty was sexy as fuck, about 5'4, 134 lbs; delicious looking little thang. Butter complexion with a weave that dropped down to the middle of her back. She wore a black bikini thong and top with 5 inch platform stilettos that laced up to her calves. Her body was slim, fit and her ass was small but was shaped so fuckin perfect. Her tatts were sexy as hell on her navel and back. The DJ put on the song "Stripper Bowl" by Quality Control and Migos to get hyped. She grabbed the towel off the stair as she stepped up on the stage. She walked to the pole, wiped it down, and tossed it to the side. She bounced that ass as she circled around the pole then leaped up on it and climbed herself to the top. She flipped upside down and twerked inverted on the ceiling. The crowd responded real hype, loving the show she was giving. The DJ shouted out as a reminder to the crowd to get up throw money on the stage. She flipped down to the center of the pole, locked her legs, leaned backwards and did some sit ups. Shawn got up and walked to the stage with a wad of money in his hand. Majesty saw him coming so she flipped backwards landing in the splits and twerked her ass. She looked back at him as he laced some money along her thong. He said something to her and walked away. Shawn sat back down at the table and got the attention of their waitress. He said something to her and pointed at a few dancers in particular who were standing at the bar. The waitress walked away and he turned and looked at the fellas.

"Aye, I hope y'all niggas ready to have a good time. Dez, Antonio, I hope y'all niggas don't get in trouble for going home smelling like some new booty. I aint trying to wreck no homes." Shawn said, jokingly.

"Nigga, you straight, I'm good." Antonio replied, sipping his drink.

"Desmond, you all good down there? You gone be straight going home or Ima have to call and check and make sure you all good?" Shawn asked.

"Trust me, I'm all good my nigga." Desmond replied, looking like something deep was on his mind.

"Okay cool, because um here they sexy asses come." Shawn said and looked back at the fine dancers who were walking towards their table.

While the ladies came over and Shawn purchased a couple of dances for the fellas the waitress walked up with another bottle. He handed her some money and told her to keep the change. She smiled in appreciation of the nice tip he gave her. By this time everybody was having fun drinking and getting dances. The dancers were enjoying the fact that they were getting them coins and free drinks. Across the room some dude was sitting at a table eating a steak dinner he'd ordered while his boy was getting a lap dance. In the middle of cutting him another piece of steak he noticed Shawn and paused. His eyes squinted as he stared a little longer trying to recall the face. He tapped his homeboy to get his attention.

"Aye bro, check this out." Dude number one said.

"What up doh?" Dude number two asked, hand full of ass while receiving a lap dance.

"Look…see big fella over there getting a lap dance from ole girl with the paw print on her ass?" Dude number one asked.

"Yeah, wsup with him?" Dude number two asked.

"That's that nigga that jacked me a few weeks ago." Dude number one said.

Dude number two made the dancer stop and get up off of him.

"Hold up, nigga you fa sho?" Dude number two asked, mean grimace on his face.

"Hell yeah, I know it's that nigga." Dude number one said.

"Ok well we gotta go holla at that nigga then." Dude number two said, downing his drink completely.

"Bet." Dude number one replied.

Majesty had freshened up after coming off stage and walked up and sat on Shawn's lap. He poured her a glass of Rozay, they toasted and they talked and laughed. After a couple of songs played, Majesty freaked his ass out on the edge of the booth. They had the livest booth in the club and others kept looking over there at them. After while Shawn told her to let him up so he could go take a piss real quick. He told her to give his boy a dance until he came back. He hollered over at Excel and told him to come get this dance from Majesty while he went to the restroom and he did so. Shawn walked off and headed to the restroom. After thirty seconds or so the dudes from the other side of the club walked by and grimaced Antonio as they proceeded to the restroom. They entered calmly and shut the door behind them. One of the dudes went and pissed in the stall next to Shawn. The other dude walked to the sink and washed his hands. He looked over at his boy and shut the water off as Shawn finished. Shawn low-key at both them niggaz as he was zipping his pants up. Shawn stepped to the sink and started washing his hands. He noticed ole boy was looking at him out his peripheral but didn't look back at him.

"Aye my man…you that dude that jack me and took my shit, nigga." The dude at the sink said with a look that could straight kill on his face.

"You got the wrong nigga, my nigga." Shawn replied, thinking quickly and pulse accelerating.

"Naw nigga, I got the right muthafucka." The dude replied.

Immediately Shawn blasted his ass in the mouth, knocking him into the wall. He punched him twice more in the face but got grabbed around the throat by the other dude who was at the stall. Shawn quickly slid out of that, turned around and started fucking that dude up. All three started bucking their ass off violently. By this time Antonio had got a bad feeling. He told his dancer to get up for a minute and he'll be right back. Excel knew his cousin and noticed the look on his face.

"Yo, you straight, cuz?" Excel asked.

"I don't know, dog. I'm about to find out." Antonio answered with a slight scowl on his face.

Excel told Majesty to get up for a moment and said he'll be right back. He got up and walked with Antonio. They walked in the bathroom and Antonio snapped when he seen they were getting the best of Shawn. He and Excel started beating the shit out of them dudes. Antonio threw one of them dudes through the stall and beat his ass over the toilet. Shawn got up and he and Excel beat the other guy's ass. A big wad of money fell out of the dudes pocket as he fell to the floor. Excel and Shawn saw that shit and Excel picked it up quick and stuffed it in his pocket. Shawn glanced at Excel and kept stomping the dude on the floor. Someone had alerted security and the huge bouncer's bum rushed in the restroom! They immediately broke everybody up and pulled them out of the restroom.

"That's what the fuck yo bitch ass get trying to fuck with a nigga like me you bitch ass nigga!" Shawn said as the bouncer was pushing him backwards!

"Fuck you my nigga; believe me I'm gone holla at you my nigga. Believe me!! Ima holla at all you bitch niggas!" The dude said as the other bouncer pushed him out towards the other door.

"Come holla at me then you pussy ass Bitch!" Shawn yelled, getting pushed out the back door of the club.

More bouncers rushed over to make sure no more drama jumped off. Excel, Shawn and Antonio were escorted out of the back door while the other dudes were escorted out of the front. Everybody stopped dancing and drinking and were looking like what the fuck was going on! Desmond and Timmy got up and immediately walked to the back trying to see what the fuck happened! They told the bouncers who they were with and they allowed them to leave out of the back door as well. Desmond and Timmy walked out and saw Antonio, Excel and Shawn talking real amped. Shawn had a slight stream of blood seeping down the side of his face from his eye, but he didn't even feel it.

"Nigga I should go out there and shoot all them muthafucka's! I don't know who the FUCK these hoe ass niggas think they fuckin with!" Shawn said, breathing heavy, unable to stand still.

"Dog chill, man. Ain't no reason to go out there and kill them niggas and go to jail for life. We done already beat them niggas ass; let them go." Antonio rationalized.

"Man fuck that scared shit, nigga! Fuck that shit!" Shawn passionately yelled as a vein appeared in his forehead and his jaw tightened!

"Dog, chill man; I need you to stay focus." Desmond said, looking him dead in his eye.

"Nigga, I am fuckin focus!" Shawn replied.

"No the fuck you ain't focus, nigga. Just calm down my nigga, for me dog." Desmond said.

Shawn stood there breathing heavy for a moment…and replied "Whatever man…fuck it."

"Yeah nigga you good." Desmond said as he looked at the rest of the fellas.

Excel looked at Desmond and said "Alright Cuz be safe out here; I gotta go pick up my son from around the corner at big momma house so I'll holla at y'all later."

"Oh okay Cuz, stay up out here man and hit me up tomorrow or something. Maybe we can get out and have drink or something." Desmond said as he gave Excel some dap.

Excel looked at Antonio and said "Aye Cuz, you know little Carlo's around the corner at Big Momma house."

"Aw damn I forgot about that shit, and I damn sho don't feel like riding all over the muthafuckin world tonight." Antonio replied, shaking his head with his hand over his face.

"Nigga I got you nigga, don't worry about that shit. I'll pick him up when I pick my son up and drop him off at your house." Excel said.

"Oh okay cool. You need some gas money or something?" Antonio asked.

"Naw nigga I'm straight; I got it." Excel replied.

"Okay bet." Antonio said.

"Aye wait, I thought they were staying over there all week though?" Antonio asked.

"Oh yeah I forgot lil James did tell me that. I'll still call and double check." Excel answered.

"Aight cool." Antonio replied.

"Alright my niggas I'll see y'all later." Excel said as he gave Antonio some dap.

"Alright Cuzzo be careful and let me know you made it home safe.

Shawn was standing off to the side talking to Timmy.

"Alright fellas I'll holla at yall boys later." Excel said, giving the fellas some dap.

"Alright boy, holla at you later. Stay up." Shawn said as he hawked up a luggie and spit off to the side.

"Alright my dogs we up out this bitch." Timmy said as he gave Desmond and Antonio some dap and left.

Shawn looked at Desmond to assure him. "Aye my nigga Ima still holla at you on that other tip we talked about earlier."

"Alright my dude don't forget." Desmond said and then Shawn and Timmy left.

Desmond turned to Antonio and said "Damn, I forgot we was supposed to chop it up."

"Oh we're definitely gone kick it. My mind just been in a total different place." Antonio said.

"Aye…let me ask you…Is it your love life that got you all thrown off?" Desmond asked.

"Trust me it is…and this drama that jumped off tonight didn't make it any better." Antonio replied.

"Do you love her?" Desmond asked.

"Yup" Antonio replied.

"But do you love her, love her? You know we gotta ask twice to find out the truth, truth." Desmond asked.

"Yes, I put that on everything I love I do." Antonio replied.

"Well you know what? Marry her." Desmond said.

"You know what? That has actually been on my mind strong lately. I just don't want to be disappointed." Antonio replied.

"Aye, think on it; just don't let her slip by if you feel she's the one for you. Quiet as kept I just bought a ring for Niya. I'm going to ask the big question tomorrow and hopefully I'll be planning a short get away to Chicago or something." Desmond said.

"Aye you never know…we might be joining yall." Antonio said, glancing at the cop car that drove by.

"Aw shit, well enough of this mushy talk. I'm out of here. Hit me up later." Desmond said, giving Antonio a pound.

"Alright bet." Antonio replied.

Desmond and Antonio headed for the car; they vigilantly looked around with every step they took. At this age ain't nobody trying to get into no drama. However you still have to be cautious…death can easily be waiting around the corner.

PEACHES DECISION

Sunday – September 15th, 2019 – Tangie House – 11am. Peaches lied on Tangie's plush couch in her den all snuggled under the cover. It was so peaceful and serene; it was the best sleep she had since she left with some of her things from Antonio's house. She moaned as she stretched and much as she could and slowly opened her eyes. She heard a little movement in the kitchen and noticed Tangie in their making coffee.

"I want some." Peaches said.

"I already knew you were about to wake up, I knew you would." Tangie said, already walking in the den with both of their cups made.

"Oh thank you boo." Peaches said as Tangie sat the hot cup down on the table.

"You welcome. Did you sleep well?" Tangie asked, sitting in a chair next to the cocktail table.

"Yeah it was better than the first few nights; I couldn't seem to relax at all. Going to sleep late and waking up too early thinking and stressing." Peaches shook her head and sipped her coffee.

"You probably just needed to clear your thoughts; I mean you have been going through a lot." Tangie said.

"A lot aint even the word." Peaches looked at her fingernail noticing it was chipped.

"How long you and Antonio been kicking it off and on? Like 10 years or something like that?" Tangie asked, sipping her coffee.

"It's going on nine years." Peaches answered.

"Nine years; that's a long time to kick it with someone even if it has been off and on. Obviously, there's a deep connection with you guys; yall just can't be wasting each other's time." Tangie said.

"So you think we're wasting each other's time?" Peaches asked.

"Yes if nothing is going to come out of yall's relationship other than just sex. Life is too short to not solidify your future. Casual sex is a momentary goal, building a solid foundation and a home along with that good sex is a life goal." Tangie said.

"Yeah, you're right." Peaches answered, thinking deeply.

"What you scared of? You're fucking the man, you're spending time with this man, you're buying shit for this man and more. Peaches do you want to be with this man?" Tangie asked, sipping her coffee.

Peaches stared out the window at the bird on the banister thinking about what Tangie just asked her and answered. "Yes"

"Peaches you didn't sound to confident when you said that... You still a commitment phobe aren't you?" Tangie asked.

"....No..." Peaches answered, looking down fiddling with her phone.

"Peaches what else is bothering you?" Tangie asked.

Peaches took a breath and answered. "DeYonte has been pursuing me heavily lately.

"I thought yall two were done with the thought of seeing each other anymore." Tangie sat back and sat her cup on the table.

"Girl we are…I mean I am…" Peaches replied.

"Peaches have yall um…." Tangie investigated, doing a sex act with her hands.

"Um anyway we met up downtown yesterday." Peaches said.

"What the? And then what?" Tangie asked, eyebrow raised.

"And…we went for a little stroll." Peaches looked around.

"A little stroll?" Tangie asked, incredulous look on her face.

"Yes a little stroll, nothing more nothing less. Then went for a ride on the people mover." Peaches replied.

"A ride? What kind of riding was you doing? Don't tell me yall did it on the people mover." Tangie said.

"Tangie, it was just a ride. However he did strongly express his feelings for me and then guess what. You aint gone believe what I'm about to tell you." Peaches said.

Tangie sat back with her eyebrow raised and speculating her ass off. "Yall fucked on the damn people mover? That's some hot Fifty Shades of Gray." Tangie said, abruptly cut off by Peaches.

"Girl ain't nobody fucked on no damn people mover." Peaches replied.

"Oh well girl you good then." Tangie said, sitting back up in her chair and sipping her coffee.

"I found out yesterday that my inbox stalker who's been sending me crazy messages and dick pics is Randy from our job." Peaches said.

"Randy?!" Tangie asked, sitting her coffee back down.

"Yes Randy." Peaches answered.

"I'm dead." Tangie flopped back in her chair in disbelief.

"Trust me I know." Peaches replied.

"You talking about creepy work Randy?!" Tangie sat back up in the chair.

"Girl yes." Peaches replied.

"Randy, Randy?" Tangie asked.

"Yes." Peaches asnswered.

"Hell nall, I'm dead again!" Tangie said, flopping back in her seat again.

"I think I may have to go to HR about this to at least put this on record." Peaches said.

"Yeah girl you gone have to and you know we have a no sexual harassment agreement in place there. They may fire his ass immediately." Tangie said, sitting up in her seat.

"I mean I ain't trying to make the brotha lose his job." Peaches said.

"Hey I rather him lose his damn job then for you to possibly lose your life because you're in constant contact with someone who's stalking you." Tangie said, getting up and sitting down next to Peaches.

"I appreciate you so much." Peaches said as they hugged.

"Hey I got your back all the way." Tangie smiled.

"Thank you so much. That's why you my ride or die." Peaches replied.

"You damn right, ride or die. Now all I need you to do is relax and go get your man." Tangie said.

Peaches looked down at her phone and noticed Antonio had text her. It read ***I love you and miss you*** and she smiled. She text him back ***I love you back and miss you more.*** Peaches got up off the couch and started folding her cover.

"What you about to do?" Tangie asked.

"I'm about to go and get my man." Peaches replied.

Facing Your Fears for Love

Antonio sipped some of his drink as he stepped to his living room window. With his two fingers he slightly pulled down on the slats of cream-colored blinds. He peered through calmly looking both ways but didn't see anyone. He sipped his drink once again and then checked the time on his watch. ***Damn where her slow ass at?*** He closed the blinds and grabbed his phone out of his pocket as he walked back into the kitchen. The phone prompted him to scan his eyes to unlock it. He clicked onto his social media page and scrolled through his friend request. ***Who the hell are all of these people sending me friend request?*** Like always its five to ten new friend request from foreigners with half naked black and white women as the profile pic. He continued to scroll past and a inbox message icon popped on his screen. A lady asked him last week if he were in a relationship and he responded ***Its complicated.*** Her recent inbox to him read ***How are you today my handsome King?*** He responded ***I'm cool dear. How are you?*** He sat his phone down and grabbed his drink. He shuffled through a few pieces of mail that was sitting on the counter. ***Oh here go my new insurance certificate! Forgot this was right here.*** He remembered he had some clothes in the washing machine that needed to go in the dryer. He sipped his drink and headed downstairs to the basement. Not even a minute later

Peaches pulled up in his driveway. She was glad they were about to talk and iron things out. She took a deep breath, looked in her rearview mirror and smiled. ***Okay girl, no more being a commitment-phobe.*** She straightened out the mirror, gathered her things and headed inside. She opened the door and walked in. She sat her purse down and a few other things on the counter. She looked around and called his name ***Tony.*** Peaches eyebrows scrunched as she noticed Antonio's phone just lying there. Her heart started beating rapidly like a criminal who was about to be caught as she quickly grabbed his phone. Immediately she tried to get into his phone but was halted by the security. Her fingers nervously typed fast as she tried to guess a couple of pass codes. ***What the fuck is this Iris Scanner?*** She noticed the phone attempted to scan her eyes and then it read no match. She put the phone directly in front of her eyes so the scanner could get a better read but again no match. She shook her head and sat his phone down. ***Niggas and these damn phone codes.*** Suddenly she thought about something… She snapped her fingers and pulled out her phone. She went into her photo gallery and pulled up a good front facial picture of Antonio. She enlarged the picture with her fingers and grabbed his phone. When the iris scan came on she put the picture from her phone up to his phone and it unlocked. ***Yes muthafucka yes!*** Immediately she went through his phone like inspector gadget mixed with CSI on steroids. She knew she only had so much time before Antonio found out she was there. She went through his text messages to see what she could find. She quickly yet carefully skimmed through different messages. She saw a couple messages back and forth between him and a couple females. It was nothing sexual, inappropriate or anything incriminating. Besides it was during the time of their separation but that wouldn't have mattered to her anyway. She immediately went to his Facebook page and clicked on his inbox. She was ready to beat somebody ass and she hadn't even read anything yet. ***Let's see what these slick hoes got to say.*** Her eyebrows scrunched as she looked at his big as list of messages. She couldn't possibly go through all of his messages in so little time. ***Damn this a bunch of damn messages. Say Hi to your new friend Diana. Say hi to your new friend Tamara. This message is from his sister. Hmmm LaRhonda, I never seen this broad. Let's see what this conversation look like.*** Her eyebrow raised as she read along. ***How are you today my handsome King? Why the fuck is this bitch talking to my man like this?! And this nigga wanna reply I'm cool dear. How are you? Really, this is what we do? These hoes is dear now?*** She heard Antonio footsteps coming up the basement stairs. She tried to click on one more juicy message to see if she could find something incriminating but found nothing of the such. Antonio walked into the kitchen to his surprise not only to see Peaches standing there but her holding his phone.

"Damn girl, you scared the shit out of me." Antonio said, startled for a second and going over to give her a hug.

"I bet you are startled." Peaches nonchalantly replied, giving him an insincere hug and two lame pats on the back.

"Okay what's wrong with you and why are you holding my phone captive?" Antonio asked, holding his hand out for his phone.

"Who is LaRhonda and why is she calling you her king and shit? What's that about?" Peaches asked with a pissed look on her face.

"She's an old friend of mine from junior high. Secondly, I never asked her to acknowledge me as King so please don't fault me for something she chose to say. And third can I please have my phone back?"

"I don't care, take your little rusty phone. You can have them hoes." Peaches replied, handing him his phone.

"How come every time you speak on women and me in the same sentence you gotta refer to them as my hoes?" Antonio asked, leaning back against the counter.

"Gone somewhere with that. I ain't stupid, I can tell when one of these hoes want my man." Peaches replied, looking at him with a straight face.

"How did you get in my phone anyway?" Antonio asked.

"Don't worry about it. You can't hide shit from me, just know that." Peaches replied, nostrils flared.

"First of all, I'm not trying to hide shit from you. Secondly, we can swap phones right now and look through em while you talking." Antonio replied.

"So why the fuck is she calling you her handsome King if you ain't trying to fuck her?" Peaches asked, side-eying him.

"I like how you just skipped over what I just said." Antonio pointed out.

"Ain't nobody's skipping over nothing. Just respond to what I asked." Peaches replied, not really wanting to swap phones yet.

"Yeah okay." Antonio replied.

"Answer my question, Antonio." Peaches retorted.

"Okay so when a man inboxes you saying hey sexy, hey ma, hey love etcetera that mean you're fucking him right?" Antonio asked, showing her the flip side of how crazy her question is.

"We not talking about me, we talking about you." Peaches replied.

"Oh so you hypocritical now?" Antonio asked.

Peaches just looked away and shook her head.

"I know what it is; yo ass just scared to be in a relationship. It's like every time we get close you find some way to generate distance." Antonio said.

"Its not that." Peaches replied.

"Then what is it?" Antonio asked.

"Its just… I don't want to get my heart broke. I don't want to get cheated on and social media don't make it no better. It's like going to a mobile club or bar every single day. And the way social media is set up a person can cheat whenever they're good and ready." Peaches shook her head.

"Babe we all been hurt, lied to, disappointed, betrayed etc. but you can't allow those things to cause you to reject the beautiful love you long for if that's what you really want." Antonio replied sincerely.

Peaches was in a slight daze thinking about what he'd just said and replied. "You're right."

"Aye…you know that true love, honesty, loyalty and that protector you say you want?" Antonio asked.

"Yes." Peaches glanced at him.

"You got it standing in front of you right now looking at you." Antonio looked straight at her.

"Right now?" Peaches replied, giving direct eye contact.

"Yes, right now." Antonio answered.

Peaches just paused and stared at him for a moment.

"Loyalty…honesty and true love huh?... What makes you feel like being this way towards me?" Peaches asked.

"Because I sincerely love you and honor you. When we were just separated all I kept thinking about was you. That short period of time without you I felt like a fish out of water. My question to you is do you need me?" Antonio asked.

"Yes, I love you, want you, and need you." Peaches answered, slowly moving towards him looking up into his eyes.

Antonio walked over to her and they slowly engaged in a deep passionate kiss.

Let's Have a Toast

Sunday – September 15th, 2019 – The Bar and Grill – 9:47pm

The bartender poured eight shots of tequila and added a lemon slice on the rim to each one. Antonio had invited some of he and Peaches close friends to the bar for a small celebration. It was Antonio, Peaches, Tangie, Desmond, Niya, Ms. Cognac, Regina and Benita. Antonio turned around and gathered their attention. He handed each one of them a shot and told him he wanted to make a toast. Antonio put one arm around Peaches and held his shot up with the other hand.

"Hey first I want to thank everybody for coming out tonight. Each one of you are very special to myself and Peaches. So at this moment I'd like to say thank you for being really good friends and in our corners. It's hard to find true friends who are pretty much like family. So here's a toast to good friendships, love, health and prosperity, Salute." Antonio said as they simultaneously downed their shots.

"Oh yeah one more thing." Antonio said getting their special attention once more. Antonio looked over at Desmond and nodded his head.

"You ready homeboy?" Antonio asked

"No doubt." Desmond replied.

Everybody looked on as Desmond reached in his pocket and pulled out a small blue case. Niya looked at his hands curiously trying to see what he was doing. ***What the fuck*** Niya thought; she just knew he wasn't about to do what she thought he was about to do. Her heart pounded like a Dr. Dre beat and her fingers waggled nervously on the table the closer he approached her. Her mouth was slightly open in awe as Desmond stepped in front of her. Everybody was just as surprised and in awe as she was. Peaches took out her phone and started video recording them.

"Niya…I love you a lot…you've been my ride or die from day one. You've been there with me through the good and the bad; I couldn't ask for a better woman in my life. So right now I'm asking you will you marry me?" Desmond asked as he got on his knee and presented his ring for her.

Niya shook her head yes and couldn't stop crying her tears of joy. Desmond put the ring on her finger and stood up and hugged her so close and deeply. Everyone clapped and was so happy for her.

"Baby I love you." Niya said, crying like a baby.

"I love you too baby." Desmond replied, trying not to cry too much.

The moment was every bit of beautiful and was the happiest moment ever in Niya's life. Antonio took out his phone and put on the video recorder. He asked Tangie to take it and start recording Peaches. Once Peaches stopped recording Antonio walked over to her and gently grabbed her hand.

"Peaches I love you more than you know. I recently found out just how much I feel like my world is incomplete without you." Antonio said, looking into her eyes.

"Antonio don't play with me." Peaches said, totally shocked yet hopeful.

"No woman has ever meant as much to me as you do." Antonio said, looking at her eyes start to water.

"Tony, I'm gone beat yo ass if you playing with me." Peaches said, tears dripping from her eyes.

"So at this moment." Antonio said, pulling a small case out of his pocket.

"Yes." Peaches answered, covering her mouth and crying and sniffling.

"Peaches will you please marry me?" Antonio asked, as Peaches jumped up on him like the happiest little girl in the world.

"Yes, yes, yes!" Peaches screamed and cried. Everybody in the bar was happy for them and clapping saying congratulations! The DJ put on the right music and the atmosphere was fantastic. Peaches got down off Antonio and he put the ring on her finger. He gave her a big ass kiss and hugged her like it was no tomorrow. Afterwards Niya walked over to Peaches and hugged her. They both took out their phones and took selfies with both their hands side by side showing their new wedding rings and posted them to Facebook and instagram. This night was a very special night and changed their lives forever.

"And you know what yall? For our honeymoon I want to plan the biggest Caribbean cruise and visit the different tropical islands. I want to walk on the beaches, eat all of the good ass food and drink all of them potent ass drinks while looking out over the ocean at one of Gods most beautiful creations, my wife." Antonio said.

"That would be so beautiful; I cant wait." Peaches said.

"Now you talking my kinda language right there." Desmond replied, pointing at Antonio.

"Yeah that does sound beautiful. I can hear the bongos and tropical music playing right now." Niya said.

"Hell yeah I love that type of music." Antonio replied.

"Hey Niya, Peaches, Tony; check this out. What yall think about a double Caribbean wedding?" Desmond asked.

"You mean like get married on the island?" Niya asked, excited.

"Like right off the ocean?" Peaches asked, excited as well.

"Yes, right off the gorgeous ocean." Desmond answered.

"I love it! Baby what you think about that?" Peaches asked, looking at Antonio.

"Babe it's a done deal if you with it." Antonio answered, looking back at Peaches.

"Heck yeah I'm with it; its like a dream come true." Peaches answered.

"Well yall know me, I'll start gathering all of the information tonight so we can book the trip and get the best rates." Niya said, amped.

"It's a done deal then." Desmond said.

"Hell yeah Caribbean life here we come." Antonio said with passion.

"Sheeeeiiiittt I'm definitely coming; just let me know!" Cognac said.

"My bags already packed!" Regina said, laughing yet serious.

The Very Next Day at Work

Peaches pulled up at work happy as a woman can ever feel. She had a picture of Antonio as her screen saver and kissed her phone. Her phone alerts kept going off; her new Facebook post was off the chain. She couldn't even click like on all of the congratulations that she had gotten because it was so many. She text ***I love you*** to Antonio and put her phone in her purse. She grabbed her coffee out of the center cup holder and drunk the rest of her coffee. She got out the car and headed into work; she already knew she was going to get mad love from her coworkers. Soon as she walked through the doors it was all smiles and congratulations. Peaches smiled and said thank you to everybody. She noticed Kandis walking out of the supervisors office. They cut eyes at each other as they crossed paths; the moment was uncomfortable, but Peaches didn't give a fuck. ***I hope I don't have to beat that bitch.*** Peaches kept it moving but things were troubling her thoughts and she needed to let it out. She abruptly decided to head straight to Kandis's cubical. Kandis was powering on her computer and was a little startled by Peaches surprise visit.

"Kandis I need to have a word with you woman to woman." Peaches said, stepping inside.

"Technically I don't like nobody interrupting me but I'm curious to know what you got to say to me." Kandis replied, looking at Peaches with a straight face.

"Good well let me give it to you straight with no chaser. I don't know exactly what your beef with me is but I don't get into it with women over a man that aint mine. So whatever your affairs is with DeYonte is none of my business. But what is my business is you sending my fiancé a friend request and waiving at him in his inbox." Peaches stated eloquently.

"First of all I don't know who the fuck your fiancé is." Kandis replied, looking at her snide.

"Well I find it quite ironic that you got an issue with me because you think I'm interrupting what you might have going on with DeYonte and coincidentally you just so happened to send my fiancé a friend request and waiving at him in his inbox. Seems a bit more than just a coincidence." Peaches replied, getting pissed.

"Like I said I don't know who the fuck your fiancé is so don't come checking me about shit." Kandis retorted, pissed.

"Okay play dumb if you want to; his name is Antonio. Brown skinned brotha with the beard. If you still clueless go check your messages and see who you was waiving at, at seven-fourteen pm last night and don't send him shit else." Peaches said, mean scowl on her face.

"Look get the fuck out my workspace with that bullshit. You don't want no problems this way." Kandis said, looking at her evil as hell.

"Look bitch you don't want no problems with me so I advise you to back away and find you another nigga to thirst after." Peaches replied.

"Get the fuck out my cubical because you starting to really piss me off." Kandis said, clapping her hands as she spoke.

"I don't give a fuck if you pissed off or not. You heard what the fuck I said, now I'm done." Peaches retorted and exited the cubical.

Peaches was ready to whoop Kandis ass as she walked to her cubicle. At that point she didn't give a shit if she got time off or fired. She stepped inside her cubical and noticed a teddy bear and a balloon. Attached was a card that read ***Congratulations again, Love Tangie.*** Peaches face went from a frown to a smile as she grabbed her phone to text Tangie. Suddenly she was startled.

"Congratulations boo." Tangie said, walking into Peaches cubicle and hugging her.

"Thank you, love." Peaches replied.

"How you feeling, Mrs. Antonio?" Tangie asked, sitting down in the other office chair.

"Well I was about to catch a case like five minutes ago." Peaches answered.

"Catch a case? Why?" Tangie asked.

"Because I had to check that bitch, Kandis." Peaches answered.

"What her stupid ass do now?" Tangie asked, eyebrows crinkled.

"Her ass sent Antonio and damn friend request and waiving all at him and shit in his inbox." Peaches said, with a mean face.

"What the fuck? That bitch out of line for that shit; that's how you get your ass whooped for real for real." Tangie replied.

"I'm trying to tell you." Peaches agreed sincerely.

"How you find out she did it?" Tangie asked.

"Because I went through his phone and messenger and seen the shit. All the bitch probably did was find my page and then saw that I was engaged and clicked on his page and sent him a friend request. And if she keep on with the shits she gone need to send a friend request to Swanson's Funeral Home." Peaches said.

"You is silly, but look enough about that hoe. Today is Peaches day and I got you these surprise flowers because I want you to smile. You got engaged and you smiling for all of us women who wish we were you right now." Tangie replied, smiling from ear to ear.

"Thank you Tangie; that's why I love you." Peaches said, going over and hugging Tangie.

"Hey long as my girl happy and feeling good that's all that matters right now." Tangie replied.

"I'm feeling really good on cloud nine right now. I still can't believe this is really happening. Me, Antonio, Niya and Desmond are going to Chicago this weekend to celebrate; just a quick little get away." Peaches replied, sitting back in her chair.

"I am so happy for yall. We were all stunned just watching it happen. It was so surreal like some shit you see at the movies." Tangie said, checking her text messages.

"I know right." Peaches replied.

"Okay I gotta go, the boss texting me. But first let me see that beautiful ass ring you got, girl." Tangie said. Peaches put her hand up and Tangie admired it. DeYonte had walked over to Peaches cubicle to speak to her and paused for a second. He saw them both talking about her ring and he kept going thinking to himself ***Fuck that ring***.

Tangie got up out of her chair. "Okay girl, I gotta go for real."

“Okay boo, I’ll come get with you at lunchtime.” Peaches said, looking at her text message from Antonio and smiling.

Abruptly Tangie turned around and sat back down. “Hey guess what? I forgot to tell you the juicy four, one, one!” Tangie said, excited.

“What?” Peaches, incredulous look on her face.

“You aint gone believe this.” Tangie said.

“Girl tell me!” Peaches said.

“Girl, a couple of the reps from human resources came down on the floor and fired Randy!” Tangie said.

“What the hell?! For real?” Peaches asked.

“Girl, somebody showed them your post about him inboxing you those harassing messages and sending you dick pics and they fired him. He was mad as fuck when they took his badge and made him leave.” Tangie said.

“Oh my God really?” Peaches asked.

“Oh well fuck him; he shouldn’t have been a stalking ass nigga.” Tangie said.

“Well that’s what he get for violating and disrespecting women.” Peaches replied.

“And guess what? When they walked up on him they caught him in the act sending another lady a dick pic.” Tangie said.

“What the fuck?” Peaches asked, looking disgusted.

“Okay look I gotta go.” Tangie said, quickly getting up and heading to her cubicle.

“Alright.” Peaches replied.

Peaches grabbed her phone and responded ***I love you so much*** to Antonio’s message. She got up and headed to the bathroom smiling as Antonio replied to her. She sent him many heart eyes, kissy faces and squirt emojis as she smiled at her phone while messaging. She looked at her ring and smiled as she opened the bathroom door. She walked to the sink and looked at her ring in the mirror; twirling her hand and admiring. She took a deep breath, closed her eyes and held her hand over her heart. She felt deeply in her feelings and was embracing the fact that her life was changing. She took a deep breath and opened her eyes. She was startled as fuck to see DeYonte in the mirror behind her.

"Oh my God boy you just scared the living shit out of me!!" Peaches said, turning around with her heart racing.

"I'm sorry, I'm so sorry I didn't mean to scare you baby I promise." DeYonte replied, putting his hand on her arm with compassion.

"DeYonte you can't call me baby. And what are you doing in the woman's restroom?" Peaches asked.

"I just needed to talk to you for a minute, that's all." DeYonte answered.

"DeYonte, you couldn't wait till I came out of the restroom?" Peaches just looked at him.

"Look, I just didn't want people being all in our mix." DeYonte said.

"What's on your mind?" Peaches asked.

"You know what's on my mind, Peaches. I'm hurt." DeYonte rubbed his head.

"...DeYonte look... I'm sorry you're hurt, but you already knew I had somebody." Peaches knew this would happen.

"But you also broke up from that somebody and then you got my feelings back involved. I've always liked you a lot but..." DeYonte said, deeply.

"DeYonte don't do this." Peaches said, shaking her head.

"Peaches I love you." DeYonte expressed sincerely.

"DeYonte please stop." Peaches requested, looking down and not wanting to have to deal with this.

"How can I stop a natural feeling I have no control over?" DeYonte asked.

"DeYonte you can't do this. I was wrong for hanging with you the other day. I'm sorry if I misled you; I was going through a lot, my mind was clouded, and I should've made better decisions." Peaches said.

"Peaches, what about the other thing?" DeYonte asked.

"DeYonte…I'm getting married. I need you to respect that." Peaches said firmly and walked out.

DeYonte stood there looking in the mirror in disbelief as she walked out. He took a deep breath and exhaled thinking how the fuck did he allow his feelings to get caught up like this. He stepped out of the bathroom and glanced around; he was glad no one saw him come out. He felt some type of way but wasn't shit he could do about it. He took out his phone and checked his social media feed as he headed to the break room. He was reading a pretty good post and felt like responding as he stepped to the vending machine. As he typed out his comment there were six ladies sitting at the break table talking about men being in their inboxes and his name was one of the names that was brought up. Carla was sitting next to Kandis and Danielle spreading gossip as usual stirring up drama. Bernard also stepped into the break area and that's when Carla decided to get on her bullshit. She repeatedly tapped Kandis on the leg and said ***aye y'all look look, watch this!!*** Kandis glanced at him with an irritated look and looked away. DeYonte and

Bernard were both walking in their direction and Carla stood up to confront them.

"Um excuse me gentlemen, us lovely ladies have a couple of questions for y'all if y'all don't mind. Is that alright with y'all?" Carla asked.

"Aw shit, I smell Carla the shit starter is about to do her norm and start some shit." Bernard replied.

"Whatever nigga." Carla replied, pruning her lips.

"What's your question?" DeYonte asked.

"Well DeYonte being that you in particular have been in me, Kandis and Danielle's inbox like right around the same time we just want to know why do niggas like you like to play those weak ass games like that? And just be a man and keep it real." Carla glanced at her girls and looked back at him confidently.

"Okay since you and your girls are bold enough to confront me I'll be bold enough to keep it blunt with you." DeYonte replied.

"Yes, keep it real with me; I love bluntness." Carla retorted nonchalantly.

"Well I'll start with you. Just because a man is in your inbox doesn't mean he's trying to fuck you. I inboxed you and said something to you about a comment someone left on a post that you and I both were following. Then I told you by the way your hair looked very nice in that style and left it at that. After that you took it upon yourself to send me sexual pictures and videos I never asked for. Basically, at that moment you was in my inbox on some sexual shit." DeYonte said as Carla abruptly cut him off.

"Nigga please!" Carla replied with attitude written all over her face.

"Hold on ain't no reason for me to lie, I got all the receipts in my inbox as well; so don't try to lie in front of your girls and let me finish answering your question. You asked me to keep it real so respect the realness. So after you sent me the sexual pics I didn't ask you for I chose to send you a dick pic. However upon having a few conversations with you I realized you had some psychological issues I didn't want to fuck with so I eased up. I never dated you, never kissed you or fucked you so I don't owe you shit. However with Kandis I felt like she was sexy and yes I did inbox her. We had a few good conversations and we decided to swap numbers and had a few cool phone conversations. However I paid attention to a few things she would post and she got some crazy outlandish expectations about men. On top of that she was always getting upset if I didn't text her first thing in the morning or right back after she text me. She started sending me a bombardment of sarcastic messages every other day falsely accusing me. She never considered if I may had been asleep or busy at work at the time and she'd send me a bunch or sarcasm and emojis and that made me back off. And it's like how are you acting like this and I'm not even your man? And then Danielle, I didn't even know she even worked here or knew y'all at all. I had a few good inbox conversations with her and then we swapped numbers. We had a few phone conversations that was cool and then I found out she had seven young kids with multiple baby daddies but I didn't hold it against her. Even though they would be loud as a muthafucka sounding like Romper room I didn't hold it against her either. It was after she told me her two oldest sons stole some money and jewelry from her brother which is their blood uncle I backed the fuck off from trying to get to know her on a dating level. I know if her kids will steal from their own uncle it's a great chance they will steal from me and thievery is something I don't do; I work too hard for my shit." DeYonte expressed eloquently.

"Well Ima be flat out with all y'all. I don't know Danielle because she hasn't been working in this department for long. Kandis I think she sexy and I was trying to see if she was feeling me and if she was I was going to try to fuck. And you Carla...you ALWAYS putting yourself out there sexually on social media like you need some dick. Therefore, I was in your inbox trying to give you some dick. You always posting pictures showing titties and ass but making post checking niggas about only wanting to fuck and wasting women's time. The problem is you are only good enough to fuck but ain't no nigga finna wife you. Why the fuck would a nigga want to date a woman who bust her titties and ass open for every nigga on social media to see? He'll be the laughing stock of the internet. You not wife material, you just fuck material. I just need to fuck and we both get a nut and go our separate ways." Bernard expressed.

Carla was offended by their bluntness and replied. "Fuck both of y'all."

"Look you asked us to keep it real and you can't take it. Bottomline is you have multiple types of men out here and women such as yourself will try to get the answer for all men from one or two different men. End of discussion." DeYonte said and walked off.

Carla was appalled and Danielle and Kandis were stunned.

"Fuck you DeYonte...and fuck you too Bernard. I wouldn't fuck yo ass no way." Carla stood there looking at them with the stank face.

A Lovely Day at the Navy Pier

Saturday, September 21st, 2019, Chicago Illinois, Navy Pier. The day was gorgeous, and people were everywhere enjoying the activities at the pier. Music played just outside the Billy Goat Tavern as people danced along the walkway. The Chicago step had people on the sidelines admiring. Antonio, Peaches, Desmond and Niya were amongst those people and decided to join in. The moment was lit and everyone was feeling good moving in sync. The vibe was magical and guaranteed to be a moment to be remembered. Once they were finished dancing they sat down at the outside table and ordered some food. Antonio felt good, clapped his hands together excitingly and asked "SO.....how are y'all enjoying life here in Chicago?"

"I'm loving it!" Niya replied.

"I'm enjoying it too. I love my Detroit City, but it feels so good to get away to another city, another state. See some new scenery, new faces, and different attractions. Oh, and most of all enjoying every bit of it with my husband to be, my boo." Peaches said, grabbing Antonio's hand and smiling.

"Well I'm definitely enjoying my new life with my Queen. I'm enjoying the siteseeing, the good food and drinks. It just takes your mind away from work, all of the day to day drama, and all this presidential Donald Trump bullshit that's been all in the news lately. I'm ready for some delicious food, and afterwards I'm ready to do some speed boating out there on the Pier." Desmond said, looking around at the speed boat bouncing across the water.

"Now that's what I'm talking about right there." Antonio replied.

"Hey, y'all excuse me; I have to go to the ladies room." Peaches said as she grabbed her purse and got up.

"I'll go with you." Niya said as she grabbed her purse as well and went with her.

Their heels clicked across the concrete as they walked to the restroom looking sexy and fly as it gets. Peaches's cell phone vibrated and she checked it. She sighed out of frustration ***Can you please stop fuckin texting me?*** She put her phone back in her purse and kept moving. Her cell phone rang again ***Oh nigga please; you aint about to keep harassing me after I done told yo ass***... she paused and calmed down once she looked at her phone and saw that it was Marlo so she answered it.

"Wsup girl?" Peaches asked as she walked through the restroom door.

"Wsup girl, how you enjoying the engaged life and Chi-Town?" Marlo asked.

"Oh, I'm loving it. Right now we are at the Navy Pier about to eat at the Billy Goat Tavern. Then after that we are going speed boating." Peaches said as she walked to the sink and fixed her hair.

Niya went into the stall to pee.

"How that skank, Niya enjoying herself?" Marlo asked, being funny.

"She's loving it." Peaches answered.

"Who that, Marlo?" Niya asked

"Marlo just called you a skank, Niya." Peaches said, laughing.

"Tell that scallywag to shut the hell up." Niya replied, smiling.

"Niya said shut yo stank ass up you raggedy trick." Peaches said.

"I aint say all that." Niya said, giggling.

"Y'all better bring me back a souvenir." Marlo said.

"You already know we got you." Peaches replied, pulling out her peach lip stick and applying some.

"Hey.....I don't mean to be all in y'all business but, can you and Antonio afford all of that y'all are doing? Last time me and you talked things were kind of tight moneywise." Marlo asked.

"Oh um...we good, yep we good." Peaches replied.

"You sure?" Marlo asked.

"We good. How's Shawn doing anyway?" Peaches asked.

"He's still running in the streets trying to get money instead of getting a legit, straight up job." Marlo replied.

Peaches heard Shawn in the background through the phone. She figured he must of overheard what Marlo said about him because she heard them start arguing.

"Well, look girl Ima let you handle your family matters. I don't want to be the cause of y'alls argument especially over no money. So Ima call you back girl." Peaches said and quickly hung up.

"I hope they be alright. You know Shawn is an obnoxious fool a lot of times." Niya said as she got up and flushed the toilet.

"Hey well that's on her, and she aint leaving him either." Peaches said while observing herself in the mirror.

Niya exited the stall and replied as she walked over to wash her hands "Well, I don't know what she see's in him and why she dont get a better man that's worth something."

Peaches phone vibrated and she looked at it. She just closed her eyes and shook her head.

"Hey…let me ask you something… Are you straight?" Niya asked as she looked over at Peaches.

"…yeah… What made you ask that?" Peaches asked looked a tad bit uncomfortable.

"Um nothing too major. It's just when you got that text earlier you looked like something was troubling you."

Peaches sort of froze because it felt like Niya could easily read her like an elementary book. Peaches had discomfort written all over her face. Niya recognized it and really became curious and concerned.

"Peaches, what's wrong?" Niya asked, seriously wondering what the heck is going on.

Peaches took a breath and excelled. "Well, that person that texted me is my coworker. And…."

Niya looked at her waiting for her to finish her sentence. Niya gestured her hands and asked "Okay, and what? Peaches are you seeing somebody and you just got engaged?"

"No." Peaches replied.

"Okay, well what's going on between y'all?" Niya asked, impatiently wanting her to finish what she was saying.

"Well…he is someone I had been seeing off and on before me and Antonio actually got engaged…" Peaches shamefully expressed.

"Peaches! You been cheating on Antonio?" Niya asked.

"Niya…you making me feel horrible." Peaches replied guiltfully.

"I'm not trying to make you feel horrible. I just recognized that this is something incredibly serious that my friend is going through and I'm trying to help you figure this out." Niya sincerely replied.

"Okay well it was just a friend's with benefits type of relationship just before Antonio and I started back taking our relationship really really serious. I really didn't exactly know, I wasn't expecting it and I didn't think it mattered. And DeYonte was just a good fuck for the time being and I was good with that. I wasn't exactly looking for a relationship. I wasn't ready to answer to anyone; I just wanted to come and go as I please without anyone contesting that." Peaches deeply expressed.

"Does this DeYonte dude know that you're engaged?" Niya asked excitedly.

"Yeah…but he just won't stop. He calls me restricted and inboxes me on social media all the time." Peaches answered, shaking her head.

"Okay here's the big question. When's the last time you fucked this guy?" Niya, hoping she didn't say no time recently.

"Like almost a week ago." Peaches hated to say.

"What the fuck?!?! Almost a week ago?! I was hoping you didn't say something like that…what were you thinking?" Niya asked, eyes wide.

"I don't know…I left work one day and…. Uh do I have to tell you everything?" Peaches asked.

"No you don't have to." Niya answered.

"Good." Peaches replied, sighing relief.

"Even though you aint right because I tell you all of my juicy shit." Niya said, making her feel guilty.

"Niya, you don't be telling me stuff about you and Desmond." Peaches said.

"I'm not telling you to tell me juicy stuff about you and Antonio. This other dude aint your soon to be husband...but that's okay you don't have to tell me." Niya said, using reverse psychology.

"Don't be trying to use reverse psychology on me." Peaches replied.

"Okay then don't tell me." Niya said, shrugging her shoulders nonchalantly.

"Okay then damn, I'll tell you! Get on my nerves." Peaches said, knowing she wanted to spill the beans to her anyway.

"Girl bye, talk to ya girl; I'm all ears." Niya said, being silly....

"Okay so I was just getting ready to leave work and...." Peaches, telling Niya exactly how it happened.

Peaches Confession

Thursday - September 12th, 2019 – Downtown Detroit Michigan – Quicken Loans Call Center 6:27 p.m – After Work Affair.

Peaches headed to her cubical to straighten it up and grab her belongings so she could go take care of some business. The afterwork affair was pretty much over and she was rushing. It had been a long day and she was so ready to go. DeYonte walked up to her cubical and looked in. ***Damn Peaches you are so damn sexy.***

Peaches closed everything up, got up out of her seat and pushed it up under the desk. She turned around and said ***Thank you, DeYonte***. He smiled and replied ***You're welcome baby. What won't I do for you my baby?*** Peaches just looked at him and shook her head.

"Always charming a sista…but you know I can't go there." Peaches said, feeling some kinda way.

DeYonte grabbed her hand. "I don't see why not; ain't no ring on your finger. Last time I checked you said you were unsure about things and wanted to remain single and gather your thoughts. Next thing I know you acting like it was no hope for us. And even though you won't say it I know you love me."

Peaches took a deep breath…she slowly pulled back her hand and said. "No I don't, DeYonte. Don't say that."

"Listen to you; you don't even believe that your damn self." DeYonte said, smiling with love in his eyes.

"Don't try to run game on me, it's not working." Peaches replied.

"Let's go hang out somewhere and enjoy the rest of the evening." DeYonte suggested.

"No DeYonte, plus I have somewhere I have to get to right now." Peaches answered.

"I'll make it a night you'll never forget." DeYonte grabbed her hand and kissed it.

"DeYonte stop it; look I gotta go, I'll see you later." Peaches said, turning and walked away.

"Okay see you later baby." DeYonte replied.

DeYonte looked at her ass in her beautiful red dress and shook his head and said. "Mmm mmm mmm you look so damn delicious in that sexy red dress, baby."

"Stop looking at my ass, DeYonte." Peaches replied without looking back and kept walking out.

DeYonte wanted to bend that ass over, sniff her pheromones and suck her lower chakra through her vaginal lips. He took a deep breath and headed on back to his desk and checking his cellphone. Casandra the receptionist saw him walking past her desk and got his attention.

"Hey DeYonte." Cassandra said.

DeYonte looked over at Cassandra and answered "Oh hey babe what's up?"

"Where yo boo go? She still here?" Cassandra asked.

"Who? Oh she just left. Why what's up?" DeYonte asked.

"Why don't you catch her and give her her phone. She was standing up here about twenty minutes ago and left it on the counter by mistake." Cassandra said, grabbing Peaches cellphone from in the drawer and handed it to him.

DeYonte took the phone and said "Okay, let me try to catch her."

DeYonte walked to his desk quickly and shut his computer off. He hurried and grabbed his keys and left. He quickly walked through the hallway; you could hear the sound of his dress shoes as he stepped swiftly. Got to the elevator and hit the button going down. The door opened immediately and he got on hitting the down button multiple times. Once the elevator stopped and the doors opened he made his way out of the back door. He was trying to catch her before she got on the transportation shuttle that takes employees from the job site to the parking garage where their cars are parked. He looked around and there was no sign of her anywhere; he was too late. He figured eventually she'd find out he had her phone as soon as she calls Casandra and she'll come get it. Almost twenty minutes later she went to reach in her purse for her phone but didn't feel it. She swiftly fingered her way through her purse hoping she didn't leave it. ***Damn, please tell me I didn't leave my damn phone at work...*** She pulled over to the side of the road and parked. She flipped through her purse a couple more times and finally accepted that she'd left it. She glanced at her empty cup holder and then tried to recall her steps. ***Damn, did I drop it? I know I cleaned off my desk and I'm sure I didn't leave it in my drawer. What the Fuck, damn.*** She immediately picked up her car phone and called up to her job. ***Come on Cassandra answer the damn phone girl.***

"Hello?" Cassandra answered.

"Hey Cassandra, this Peaches." Peaches said.

"Oh hey girl. You know you left your phone up here." Cassandra said.

"Okay cool, I kind of figured that. I'll be back up there in about fifteen to twenty minutes to get it." Peaches replied, staring at this guy with his shirt off who was jogging by.

"Oh girl I don't have it; DeYonte has it." Cassandra said, hoping she wouldn't be mad.

"DeYonte got it?! What the hell is DeYonte doing with my phone?" Peaches asked, not wanting him to be trying to pry in her phone.

"You had pretty much just walked out and I gave him your phone to hurry up and give to you before you left. He never came back so I figured he'd given it to you." Cassandra answered.

"Oh Damn Cassandra…" Peaches replied, flopping back in her seat and running her fingers stressfully through her hair.

"I'm sorry boo I was just trying to get you your phone." Cassandra felt bad, hoping she didn't get Peaches in any trouble.

"It's cool, don't sweat it boo; I'll get it." Peaches replied.

"Oh okay…you know I'm feeling kind of bad right now." Cassandra feeling guilty in the hot seat.

"Sandy, you good boo; I'll get it." Peaches assured.

"Oh okay cool, well call me if you need me." Cassandra replied, ready to get off the phone so she could stop feeling horrible.

"Okay boo, let me um call you back." Peaches said, frantically.

"Okay talk to you later." Cassandra said and hung up the phone.

All Peaches could think of was Antonio out of the blue calling her phone and DeYonte answering it. She put her car in drive and headed across town to DeYonte's townhouse. She tried not to whip through traffic too reckless; didn't want to get stopped by the police. She didn't know DeYonte's number by heart to call him directly. She started to call her own phone from the car phone but realized that wouldn't be a wise idea. She didn't want him to have any of her other phone numbers. She hopped on the freeway and weaved her way through traffic like a Nascar driver. It seemed like everybody who was on the road were driving like fuckin idiots. ***How the fuck did these non-driving ass bitches get a fuckin licenses?*** She was thinking of all kind of lies just in case Antonio called her phone and he answered. After almost about twenty minutes of whipping through traffic she finally arrived at his street. It seemed like she just couldn't get to Demonte's townhouse fast enough. She pulled up into his complex and drove around to where he lived. ***Lord please let this man be here.*** She tried to look up through his picture window to see if she could see him. She pulled up into his parking spot just in front of his garage door. She checked her hair in the rearview mirror to make sure she wasn't looking a mess. She got out the car and looked around as she headed to the door. She rang the doorbell and knocked on the door like she was the F.B.I. DeYonte was upstairs on the third floor in his bedroom when he heard the doorbell ring. He didn't even look outside, he already knew it was her. He had just finished showering minutes before she got there. He tossed on some shorts real quick and headed down to open the door. She rang the doorbell and knocked on the door once again. ***Dammit where the fuck is he?!*** She decided to go to the car and call her own phone with a blocked I.D. As soon as she grabbed her car door handle she heard his front door open. She turned around and he was there in the door smiling at her.

"Hey pumpkin, I thought you were the police by the way you were knocking on the door." DeYonte said, sarcastic.

"Boy, were you in there sleep or something? And where is your clothes at? Ain't nobody trying to look at your naked ass." Peaches remotely locked her car.

"Well I just got out the shower and you were beating on the door. So I hurried up and just threw on some shorts, rushed down three floors, two flights of stairs just to answer the door for you. Is that a good enough reason for you my dear?" DeYonte asked sarcastically, shutting the door behind her as she stepped in.

She shook her head ***Ole sarcastic ass.*** "Negro, where's my phone at?"

"It's upstairs safe on my kitchen counter." DeYonte answered as he led her upstairs.

Peaches just looked at him for a second and then followed him upstairs. She stared at his ass and how the muscles flexed in his calves with every step. She closed her eyes and shook her head thinking to herself. ***I'd sniff the shit out of his balls and suck his dick if things were different.*** They made it up the stairs and headed for the kitchen. She stopped in the living room and admired the artwork that he had hanging up on his walls. She found them fascinating so she walked over for a closer look.

"I love black and white art, especially black and white oil paintings and charcoal drawings. This one here is so unbelievable; just look at the detail. Wow absolutely amazing." Peaches deeply expressed.

DeYonte walked into the dining room with her phone, corkscrew and a bottle of Moet. He sat the stuff down on the beautiful dining room table.

"Yes the title of that piece is called "Survival". It was done by an artist named Men-Tal." DeYonte replied, grabbing a couple of champagne glasses out of the china cabinet.

"I love it." Peaches said, turning around and looking at him.

"Thank you." DeYonte replied, popping the cork on the champagne.

The champagne bubbled up to the top and spilled on the table a little bit as he filled the glasses.

"Look at you making a mess." Peaches said, naturally wanting to wipe up the mess with a paper towel.

"Yeah, my bad." DeYonte said, smiling.

"Wait a minute, hold up. What am I thinking? Boy, go put on a shirt." Peaches expressed, glancing at his dick print and immediately looked away.

"Oh I'm sorry if I offended your eyes... Even though we've explored each other's bodies over and over." DeYonte replied, laying it on smoothly.

"Look, I gotta go so let me just get my phone and leave." Peaches said, dropping her keys to the floor as she reached to grab her phone.

At that point he knew something wasn't right with her. It seemed like she'd been thrown off of her square pretty much all day.

"Look whatever you're going through today I want you to relax. Please understand that there's nothing in this world that will stop me from being there for you. I know you...and I know when something's troubling you. When I walked up to you at your desk you looked like you were about to jump through the ceiling as if you saw a ghost. Then you couldn't find your keys, looking all over the place when actually you left them up front at work. Then you dart out of work like forty going north and left your cell phone. Now do you care to share what's on your mind?" DeYonte asked, handing her the glass of champagne.

"I've just been stressing and it's um…it's been having my thoughts kind of cloudy these last few days." Peaches answered.

DeYonte reached for her shoulder and she stopped him by grabbing his hand and asked, "What are you doing?"

"Will you just relax? You already know I'm a massage therapist. One of the things a massage therapist does is alleviate stress and tension which happens to affect your thinking. Like how your mind has been cloudy and you forgetting stuff… I'm just trying to feel how tense you are." DeYonte calmly replied making her feel at ease.

She loosened his hand and he calmly placed his hand on her shoulder. She closed her eyes and embraced the utopian touch of his hand firmly squeezing that tense shoulder muscle. The feeling was so good the only thing better left to do would be bust an explosive nut and take a good undisturbed nap.

"Woman your shoulder muscle feels like a damn brick." DeYonte expressed with sincerity.

"I know, I know, and I hate to admit it, but I swear to God that felt really good." Peaches deeply replied.

DeYonte grabbed one of the living room chairs and a leather foot stool and pulled them close.

"Have a seat." DeYonte told her.

"No, no DeYonte I can't." Peaches said reluctantly.

"Peaches have a damn seat woman. You already said my hand felt like paradise and your shoulder feels like a damn brick. You know damn well you need this so just relax…sit down and allow me to do what I do best and make you feel better." DeYonte sipped his champagne.

Peaches looked at him for a second trying to read through him but couldn't. She knew basically she was more so playing the role of not wanting the massage. ***Okay fuck it. What the hell? I'm not married, and it aint nothing but a massage that I do need very badly. It's only one time anyway.*** She turned up her glass of champagne and downed it. She grabbed the bottle, poured her another glass and then sat her ass down like he told her. She took a very nice sip and then relaxed. DeYonte walked up behind the chair and with both hands and gently started squeezing her shoulders. She slowly tilted her head to the side to stretch the muscle where he was massaging. He asked her ***Where do you feel the soreness mostly?*** And she replied ***I feel it really bad in my left shoulder and back.*** He took both of his hands and massaged her left shoulder passionately. It was the perfect example of pleasure and pain. The simultaneous feeling was irresistible especially since she was sexually attracted to him. This sensational she felt each time he squeezed her muscle made her moan with languish. Her body language spoke volumes of how she was truly embracing it. He knew she was loving it just as much as she was needing it. The touch was loving and caring secretly stimulating vaginal condensation. He leaned over and kissed her at the tip of her forehead. She leaned her head back and grabbed his arm sensually. He gently kissed her nose and softly kissed her lips. The light dry kiss turned into the succulent suck of their bottom lips. Their tongues touched as his hand eased down to her breast with his finger rotating her areola. Her lips were so plump and soft as they kissed making his dick harder and harder. Her hands caressed his bald head ***Got dammit how did I get myself into this? Fuck it, I'm not married and it's only one last time for ole time sake. Who's gonna know?*** Every guard she had built up was alleviated and compromised. He really liked her for a long time and realized he loved her when she basically moved on. His heart melted with every kiss and her vaginal scent was compelling to him. All dogs were officially off the chain and all lust must be fulfilled. She pulled him around in front of her and kissed and nibbled his bulging hard dick through his shorts. She wanted him to flat out fuck her damn mouth like a trifling whore who tried to steal from him. He unloosened his shorts and pulled out a fully erect eight inch pretty dick. She grabbed his dick and joyfully sniffed his balls; feeding her sudden appetite for giving him a blow job. She rubbed his warm dick all over her face and then placed the head in her mouth. She sucked like she was trying to suck a thick shake threw a straw while stroking his shaft. He gently ran his fingers through her hair and lightly palmed her head making her go deeper. So indeed, she did; she opened her mouth wide and deep throated his dick with her eyes squinted tight. She then started giving him the best passionate head he had ever felt. She took his dick and lathered his balls with her tongue. She held his shaft upright and licked from his nuts all the way up the vein to his plump dick head. She twirled her tongue around the rim and succulently sucked the rim of that plump mushroom. She pleasurably enjoyed every moment of it; her eyes were closed as she moaned. She sucked like she was trying to win a million dollars making him want to shoot cum all in her warm wet mouth. She made sloppy sound affects as saliva spilled from her big lips! She flicked and dabbed her tongue on his pee hole with a thick string of saliva connected from the head to her mouth. DeYonte couldn't take that shit no fuckin more!!! He picked her up gripping her ass and carried her up the stairs. She held his face sensually tongue kissing him all the way to his bedroom. The buildup was intense and the kissing became fierce! Fuck this shit he needed to take full advantage of that ass that slightly bubbled out all day at work. She wanted to be taken full advantage of! He put her down and aggressively turned her around in a frisking position up against the bed. He smacked that ass and she loved the sting. He raised her dress and threw her right leg up on the bed! Pussy and ass wide open he stepped closer and fit his dick right in. It was pure ecstasy with him all up on her ass with a stiff dick massaging her vaginal walls. He held her leg up and gripped her shoulder with the other hand stroking her good. He turned her over on the edge of the bed and placed her feet on his chest. She clawed his strong masculine arms tightly as he repeatedly drilled her pussy like he was pissed the fuck off at her. They breathed intensely as pleasure, chemistry and lust was evoking a climax so damn extreme! She locked her legs around his neck and he gripped her shoulders with both hands! She squinted her eyes tight, gripped the sheets and started smacking the bed with her other hand!! She squirted all on that fucking Dick and tried to push away because it felt like her soul drained out. Cum percolated all through his dick; he couldn't hold back no damn longer!! He pulled out and jacked his shaft making cum shoot all the way to her neck. He squeezed out more on her stomach and pussy. They both breathed heavily and didn't want to move as their bodies quivered from the shock of cumming so hard. DeYonte went into the restroom to get a warm cloth to wipe her off. While he was gone, she laid there punishing herself with her thoughts. She went from feeling incredible utopia to the burden of guilt and conviction. She felt terrible because she knew her and Antonio were getting engaged in months to come.

However it was no turning back; what was done was done, now deal with it….

Back At the Navy Pier – Chicago Illinois

Niya stood there in the ladies room talking to Peaches floored by what she had just told her. Niya didn't exactly know how to respond as she stood there with her hand on her hip and mouth slightly opened. Peaches looked at Niya feeling guilty and embarrassment.

"I know that shit sound crazy don't it? Don't make me feel more horrible than I already do. I've been trying my best to forget that it even happened. I swear after that moment I've never stepped out and have been one hundred percent devoted to my man only. Why you looking like that?" Peaches asked, wondering what Niya's response would be.

"Damn girl I don't know if I should tell you how risky and crazy that shit was you did or if I should go and fuck my man over the railing of the Navy Pier because that shit did sound steamy and hot." Niya said, hilariously yet shocked.

"Uh thanks boo for your positive understanding. Now I really feel horrible." Peaches said sarcastically.

"Peaches you know I'm a therapist and I deal with these types of matters almost every single time.

"Okay my bad but look...all that's in the past and this is a new day. We all make bad decisions that burden our thoughts and weigh heavy on our hearts. Now you said you haven't stepped out on him since and that's excellent. You guys are engaged now and we will not have any more beat Peaches up parties okay? Everybody knows you're a good loving woman, so let's leave the past in the past and let's get back out there to our men before they get to worrying about where we are." Niya said.

"Okay." Peaches replied, taking a deep breath.

"Aye...just one more thing..." Niya said.

"What?" Peaches asked with eyebrow raised.

"Are you still a commitment-phobe?" Niya asked.

"...I mean...nall..." Peaches replied, unsure.

"Trust me when I tell you this I want nothing but the best for you and Antonio. I want y'all to get married, marriage is sacred...and if you take those vows and you say I do to that man then I want you to mean it. Don't let your inbox destroy your beautiful future." Niya said as they headed back to their significant others.

In the meantime back at the table Antonio and Desmond were having a little cousin to cousin talk. The waitress brought the drinks they had ordered. Antonio took a sip of his drink and decided to share his thoughts with Desmond.

"Aye bro I want to tell you something." Antonio said with a straight face."

"I'm all ears, Cuzzo." Desmond replied.

"You ever cheat on your ole lady?" Antonio asked.

"Huh?" Desmond asked, not expecting that question.

"Have you ever cheated on your Niya?" Antonio asked again.

"Yeah I hear you; you just caught me off guard with that question. But um...to answer your question yeah I did in the beginning. I mean...what made you ask a question like that?" Desmond asked, curiously.

"I ask because from time to time Peaches will say to me all men cheat. My thing is if you feel all men cheat then why the hell do you date me expecting me to be faithful if you honestly believe all men cheat? That shit just don't make sense to me." Antonio replied.

"Well my brotha that's because all men cheat bruh. You a man, why you acting like you don't know this, bro?" Desmond asked.

"Bro, you sound like God designed men to cheat by default." Antonio replied, looking at the couple zip by on roller skates.

"Aye man I'm just saying." Desmond replied.

"Bro, really your logic is scaring me." Antonio replied.

"Bro, so you telling me you never cheated on Peaches?" Desmond asked.

"Brotha not only have I not cheated but I have no desire to. However it's alarming that you sincerely believe that it is virtually impossible for men to be faithful to a woman. And this also shows me that many of us men have been bread to insatiably run through women." Antonio stated.

"Dog I do not believe that." Desmond looked at him sideways.

"Bro let me give you my ingredients to be faithful. Really pay attention to a woman when you first meet her. Make sure she epitomizes everything that lights your fire in a woman physically. If you like a woman with a fat ass make sure she got a fat ass. If you like long hair, short hair, afro, weave, brown skin, light skin, thick lips, round hips etc. If that's what you're attracted to then make sure she has that. Get to know her by having great conversation with her without sex being the focal point. That way you get to see where her head is at and make sure yall are compatible mentally. Make sure yall standards are parallel but you'll only get to know this by having good conversation." Antonio said.

"So you're like the guardian angel of faithfulness I suppose?" Desmond asked sarcastically.

"Oh and if you're a freak and like to do freaky shit then make sure she's into that same freaky shit or open to explore new things sexually." Antonio said.

"Okay you should put that in a book titled the forty-eight Laws of Faithfulness by Antonio aka Jesus Jr." Desmond said, sarcastically.

"Oh you got joke jokes." Antonio replied.

"Yeah but right now we gone change the subject, the ladies coming. So what you think our Detroit Lions gone do this season?" Desmond asked, abruptly switching the conversation.

"Mark my words, the Lions are going to make some noise. Matt Patricia is building a team that can run the NFC. But you know the politics, Lions get cheated every year." Antonio replied.

"What them Pistons gone do this year?" Desmond asked.

"Well we still got Blake Griffin and Andre Drummond and we finally got some good bench players so we going to the playoffs. If Derick Rose and Joe Johnson can be anything like their old selves and the bench do their part the Pistons will be a serious problem especially with LeBron being in the west. Plus DeWayne Casey is excellent at developing talent in his players." Antonio expressed confidently.

"And speaking of LeBron; he's definitely the greatest of all time." Desmond said.

"And speaking of drug abuse you must be on something because you sound insane. LeBron will never equal or surpass Jordan's greatness. Number two, he's not even better than Kobe." Antonio stressed before Desmond cut him off.

"Nigga you crazy, LeBron will kill Kobe!" Desmond replied, animated.

"See, what yall little LeBron-sexuals never want to admit is every time LeBron won a ring he constructed a Super team to do it. Kobe never did that weak shit; he worked with what he had." Antonio pointed out.

"Um Kobe had Shaq! Did you forget about them?" Desmond said.

"Yeah but Kobe was drafted by Charlotte and traded to the Lakers as a rookie if I'm correct. It just so happened the Lakers ended up with Shaq; that's not Kobe's fault. Kobe didn't need to go out and recruit the captains of two different teams to unite them on one team in order to win a championship like LeBron did with D-Wade and Chris Bosh." Antonio said.

"Man you trippin." Desmond replied.

"You know what's funny? Yall LeBron loyalist are so hypocritical that yall will excuse the fact that LeBron left Cleveland because he felt like he couldn't win and united a Super Team in Miami, but yall have the nerve to talk shit about Kevin Durrant going Golden State. Yall logic is just void when it comes to Bron. How do yall do that?" Antonio asked being sarcastic.

"Aye man LeBron is the G.O.A.T." Desmond said.

"And oh yeah, don't think just because LeBron is in a Lakers jersey and got Anthony Davis that they automatically gone beat the L. A Clippers or the Rockets." Antonio said.

"Nigga you crazy!" Desmond replied

"And I bet you start to see the NBA media continue trying get every good free agent available to go play with LeBron. I bet you that hoe shit happen." Antonio replied.

"Nigga, as long as LeBron is healthy the Lakers will beat the Clippers, Golden State, the Rockets and the entire West this season." Desmond said, turning his drink all the way up and downing it.

"How much you want to bet? Matter of fact they play on Christmas day. Put your money where your mouth is." Antonio said, downing the rest of his drink.

By that time the ladies were approaching the table.

"Oh hell nall, how y'all gone have a toast without us?" Peaches asked, sitting down in her seat.

"See, how they doing us already, girl? Before we got engaged they acted just right. Now that they put a ring on our finger they can act out. This is why we have to establish Lady Law and have them serve us on hands and feet until they learn how to act." Niya said, high-fiving Peaches.

The waitress returned to the table with their food looking absolutely delicious. She placed their plates before them, told them to let her know if they needed anything else, and left.

"Hey look, before we dig into this delicious looking food I want to have a toast. A toast to having happy relationships for the rest of our lives. Let us be prosperous for the rest of two-thousand- nineteen, and all the years to come and have an overabundance of dirty sex." Desmond said.

"I want to thank my Creator for my better half, my future husband…my King for making me the happiest woman on the planet. I love you so much." Niya said as she wiped a tear from her eye.

Desmond put his arm around her, pulled her closer and kissed her forehead.

"Aw, y'all about to make me cry. But hold on because I also want to toast to me being not afraid…not being afraid of commitment anymore and being with the one who completes me." Peaches said, with a smile as she looked at Antonio.

"Well, I want to have a toast to me having the woman of my dreams. The lady who completes me in so many ways and helps keep me on my feet. And I'm so glad I aint got one of them wives who decides to start slacking on the sex and holding back the cookies after I asked her to marry me, SALUTE!!" Antonio said, being funny.

"You are a nut, but sadly that is so true in many cases. Yes, glad we aint got them problems." Desmond said, playfully.

"Well I'm going on a sex strike in the next thirty minutes." Peaches said playfully.

"Well I'm going to the strip club in the next forty-five minutes; holla." Antonio replied, being funny.

"Oh you funny, funny." Peaches replied, looking at Antonio.

"Aye, just switching the subject for a second. I forgot my cousin has a big-time vapor store out here called ***Smooth Vapes.*** He throwing a classy gathering there tonight and told me to have us swing through there." Antonio said.

"Who's your cousin? Have I met him before?" Peaches asked.

"My cousin Vince. You know who Vince is; he's been to some of my parties I was having when you and I first started kicking it. Matter of fact at the party you and I toasted with him because he was moving to Bentonville Arkansas to open up a business." Antonio answered.

"Oh yeah, I remember him; he's pretty cool." Peaches replied.

"Oh you talking about big fella; used to run the jewelry store in the Penobscot Building back at home, downtown. Yup I remember him. Now he's your cousin on your father's side?" Desmond asked.

"No, we're not blood cousins; we've just been great friends for a really long time; he's family to me for life." Antonio answered.

"Now what is Vapors? Is that like that hookah people be doing at the hookah bars?" Niya asked.

"Naw, this aint that. Vapors are used for a couple different reasons. Some vapors have low doses of nicotine in it too and basically helps people kick the cigarette habit. Then you have some people who just like the feel of vaping do it for the pleasure of the different flavors. Vaping is so huge now they have vape competitions." Antonio answered.

"Oh damn, he's doing it big then, huh?" Desmond asked.

"He's doing it bigger than big. What made him skyrocket over the rest of the people in the vapor business is that most people order their vapor flavors from a warehouse and have the same flavors as the next person in the business. Vince makes his own flavors that aint nobody else heard about or ever tasted before. Trust me he's the man when it comes to the vapor business. Matter of fact he started off up in Arkansas, he just moved here and opened this store out in Schaumburg Illinois.

They all laughed and saluted to having a great time in the Windy City. Before they went back home to Detroit, they wanted to partake in every activity they could. They absolutely enjoyed the Navy Pier, the Margaritaville Bar and Grill, the Billy Goat Tavern, and the speed boat ride on the Chicago River. The next day they went to Ihop, the Shedd Aquarium, and the Cheesecake Factory. After that they ended the trip off by going over to visit one of Antonio's good friend's, Mr. Blaq Ice and his wife, Toy. Ice always has a great show he puts on every Friday night called Strictly 4 the Listeners hosted by Lovely Lyricist and Poetry Tap. It was the Motown Vs Chi-town Verbal Collision Poetry Battle. It was Blaq Ice, Black Maria, Jeronimo, Men-Tal, Imani-Truth, Blk, Ju, Knowledgeborn, and many others from the P.O.E.T family putting on an unforgettable show. The next morning they got up and headed back home.

Home Sweet Home

Sunday night – September 22nd, 2019 – 8:45pm - Detroit Michigan.

The sound of pan seared salmon filets was like music to the ears as Antonio cooked for Peaches. She carefully rolled her blunt and watched in admiration as he did his thing. He sprinkled some freshly chopped rosemary over his country fried potatoes and added a little white wine then placed a lid over it. He loved the dress she had on and the way she was rocking it. It was some type of dark pinkish color with ruffles that cascaded over her breast. He glanced at how it laced tied just over her cleavage with the tassels that dangled to her navel. He was drawn to how her dress hugged her frame. The way it accentuated her small waistline and well-rounded hips was perfection. Her thick legs were so inviting as she sat there with them crossed. Her hair was laid draping down to one side and her lip stick and fingernails color coordinated beautifully. ***Damn what a gorgeous work of art*** he thought to himself. He shook his head and diced up some salad and loaded it with veggies and croutons and it was time to eat. Peaches was always impressed with his cooking skills but it feels even better when the chef is your personal lover, fiancé and friend. She wet the blunt with her tongue as she looked at him sexually. Sexual thoughts went through his mind as he grabbed a couple of white plates and a couple of wine glasses. She sealed the blunt tight as he grabbed a bottle of wine out of the refrigerator. He grabbed a candle and placed it on the extended counter just to the left of the stove. He fixed their plates and poured them both a glass of wine. He placed everything on the counter and lit the candle; dinner is served.

"Ain't nothing sexier than having your King cook for you." Peaches said as she walked over to the counter.

"You got a personal chef for life." Antonio said, lighting the candle.

"I promise I'm going to make you know that you are the King for the rest of this life." Peaches said, placing the blunt in her mouth and lighting it with the candle fire.

"Well let me know how it taste baby." Antonio said, waiting on her to take a bite of her food.

"Oh okay." Peaches replied.

Peaches was already on cloud nine and with the wine and the weed she felt even higher. She slowly reached under her dress and stuck her finger in her wetness. She exhaled weed smoke to his face and she placed the same finger in her mouth and sucked the shit out of it.

"It taste delicious Daddy." Peaches said, placing her finger back in her wetness.

"Oh really?" Antonio asked, grabbing the dinner plates and carefully moving them aside.

"Yes really." Peaches answered, placing her same finger on Antonio's mouth and rubbing it on his lips.

Antonio moved the candle out of the way and pulled Peaches close to him. They grabbed each other tightly and tongue kissed the fuck out of each other. He gripped her lower back and squeezed her fat ass with the other hand. He passionately kissed her neck as she puffed the weed and blew out smoke in ecstasy. He gently raised her dress and lifted her up on the counter. She grabbed her wine and sipped it as he kissed her stomach. Her breathing accelerated as he traced his wet tongue down her stomach to her inner thigh. He eased up and downed the last of his wine while she took a heavy toke of the blunt. She pulled him to her for a kiss and she gave him a shotgun as they passionately tongue kissed. Smoke escaped their mouths the more they kissed. She grabbed the wine bottle and poured him some more. He took a huge chug of the wine and then gently nibbled on her stomach again. She loved the way his lips felt and he could smell her delicious vaginal scent calling him. He nibbled all the way down to her inner thighs making her super moist. He softly kissed her clitoris as she closed her eyes. She moaned as he sucked it like his fucking life was on the line. She blew more weed smoke in the air loving the way his mouth felt like a miracle mixed with Hennessy as she licked it. She gripped his head and slowly fucked his face. She could tell he was turned on by it because he started licking it fiercely. She grabbed the wine bottle and hit it from the neck. Her vaginal sensation made her want to call on the Gods. She tilted the bottle and trickled wine down her stomach to her vaginal lips and his mouth. Her eyes rolled upward and her mouth opened from the incredible feeling. She was about to explode and he wasn't stopping. She moaned louder as her body tightened from the feeling. She screamed and dropped her wine glass on the floor as it shattered off to the side as she climaxed. Her vaginal juices saturated his beard so wet. He lifted her up as she wrapped her arms around his neck and her legs around his waist as he carried her up the stairs. She sucked and licked his neck with every step as she held him tightly. Once they made it to the room he laid her back on the bed and kissed her once more. He eased her up and carefully took off her dress. He walked to the closet, fumbling around on the top shelf in the dark. He grabbed the two mask, a black leather choker along with a dog leash, a bag of items and walked back over to the bed. He handed her a mask; it was like a silk ski mask with the mouth open. She slid the mask over her face and fastened the choker around her neck. She felt like his lascivious sex slave and she loved it. He put on the black phantom mask representing his dominance. She took one final puff of her blunt and got up and sat it in the ashtray on the dresser. She walked over to him and licked his mask as she unfastened his belt and unzipped his pants. She reached in his briefs pulled out his manhood. She kneeled and began slapping herself in the face with her King's dick. She twirled her tongue around the head and succulently appeased his oral fixation. She slowly suctioned the tip tight with her lips and slowly forced it down her throat. The vein surfaced in her neck from swallowing his shaft as much as she possibly could. She took it out so she could finally breathe and put it back in her mouth doing it again. She put his hands on her head and she gripped his legs making him fuck the dog shit out of her face. She swallowed his dick once again and shook her head trying to swallow every inch as much as she could. She took it out and grabbed the dog leash and latched it onto her choker. She snatched it tightly and handed him the other end. She got down on her hands and knees with her ass butterflied in the air. She slow winded and seduced him like a deviant seductress. He pulled on the leash and she crawled over to him like a filthy sex slave. She kissed his feet, and licked his leg tracing her tongue up his inner thigh. She rolled her face all in his dick and nuts, lathering his shaft with her saliva. He tugged on the leash again and she hopped up on the bed doggy-style and arched her fat booty up perfectly. He grabbed her ass cheeks and spread them wide open and passionately tongue kissed and sucked her peach again. He slid his hand in the bag and pulled out a bullet. He flicked it on and vibrated her clitoris as he licked her vaginal lips so succulent. The feeling was incredible; she tightened her fist and bit the bed sheets. Got damn she couldn't take it no more and came profusely! He loved having her fat ass smothering his face and the sweet flavor of her vaginal juice. He was so aroused he stood up and stuck his rock-solid dick inside of her and started stroking. He gripped the leash tightly, got a fist full of her hair and started pounding that ass like he was swinging a jackhammer. Her ass rippled like a title wave with every pelvic thrust. The moon light glared through the window shining on her physique so sexy. She gripped the sheets the more intense he fucked her. He leaned over and licked her back and started nibbling her waistline. He turned her over on her back and pulled her to the edge of the bed with her legs on his shoulders. She was so vulnerable as he slid it deep inside of her. Her warm, wet, tight walls felt like an erogenous utopia. She gripped the back of his head with both of her hands pulling him to her. She passionately licked and French kissed the lips of the mask as he gave her deep pelvic thrust repeatedly. Her mind was running wild as they fucked harder, and harder! Breathing intensified as he pounded deeper and deeper! He felt the cum percolating and could no longer hold it! She could tell by his breathing he was about to explode! He pulled out and she immediately dropped down to the floor on her knees. She opened her mouth wide and stuck her tongue all the way out. He blasted off nut all in her mouth and on her face. She spewed the cum down the side of her face and swallowed the rest. She wrapped her lips around the tip and grabbed his shaft jacking the rest of the cum in her mouth. Antonio laid back on the bed trying to recover from that super crazy Janet Jacme performance. Peaches wanted to smoke and eat by then.

"Baby I'm hungry as hell now. I'm about to go downstairs and heat that food up. You hungry?" Peaches asked, pulling the mask off and unfastening the dog leash.

"Hell yeah baby heat mine up too." Antonio replied.

"Okay just come down in about five minutes." Peaches slipped on his t-shirt.

Peaches headed downstairs with love on the brain. She smiled as she looked at her ring while walking into the kitchen. She grabbed the wine and the glasses then headed over to the sink and rinsed them. She looked deeply at her ring and kissed it. She looked up and was scared to fucking death noticing DeYonte's reflection in the window standing behind her! Immediately she turned around traumatized by him being there.

DeYonte quickly put his index finger up in front of his lips. "Shhhhhhh I know how this may look but trust me I'm not here to cause trouble. I just really need to talk to you."

"Talk to me?! Do you realize that you're in my fucking house with my fucking fiancé who I'm going to fucking marry?!" Peaches asked quietly, trying to hear if Antonio was coming.

"Yes I fucking realize that." DeYonte said sarcastically.

"DeYonte, you are insane. How the fuck did you get in my house?" Peaches asked.

"Do you really have to ask that? I'm a lock Smith remember?" DeYonte asked, sarcastically.

"Oh my God, I can't believe this shit. DeYonte leave now." Peaches heard Antonio getting up.

"You leave with me." DeYonte said.

"DeYonte, I'm engaged." Peaches heard the water running upstairs.

"Peaches, I'm in love with you." DeYonte replied.

"DeYonte, leave before I call the police." Peaches said.

"While you're dialing, I'll show you're fiancé our text messages." DeYonte retorted.

"DeYonte, please leave. I promise I'll call you later." Peaches pleaded, pushing him towards the back door.

"I'm not leaving unless you kiss me." DeYonte said, backing up.

"I'm not kissing you, DeYonte please leave…now." Peaches pleaded again, opening the door.

"Then I'm not leaving." DeYonte said, using his foot to keep the door open as she's pushing him out.

By this time Antonio was almost down the stairs, ***Aye babe, I'm ready for some food and round two***. Peaches was fuckin distraught as she turned around to plead her innocence! ***Baby I swear it's not what you think; I can explain.*** Antonio stepped into the kitchen with a strange look on his face.

"What is there to explain?" Antonio asked, looking at her strange.

"Baby I swear when I came down here he was here!" Peaches confessed, glancing behind her wondering where DeYonte had gone.

"What?... Babe I think you need to leave the weed alone for a little while; it got your ass talking crazy." Antonio said walking towards her.

She noticed out her peripheral that DeYonte was crouched down hiding behind the counter. He was looking up at her making faces like it was a joke.

"I'm sleepy and talking out the side of my neck." Peaches replied, walking up to Antonio and hugging him.

"Babe you don't have to be apologetic for not having some food warmed up. I'm not petty and trippin about that." Antonio said, kissing her on the forehead.
"Thank you sweetie." Peaches replied, hoping DeYonte just stayed very still and quiet.
"But I do want you to slow down on the trees a little bit." Antonio requested.
"Okay." Peaches nodded her head.
"Oh shit, speaking of trees I left the blunt upstairs lit. I'll be right back." Antonio headed upstairs
Peaches immediately rushed over to DeYonte! "DeYonte you gotta go!"
DeYonte stood up, "I told you, I'm not leaving till I get my kiss."

"I can not believe you are doing this." Peaches said, banging her fist on the wall out of frustration.

"Give me a kiss and I'll go." DeYonte smirked.

"You really want a taste of my finance, huh?" Peaches asked, referring to the dried cum on her lips while glancing behind her.

"I aint worried about that nigga doing shit to me. He dont want no smoke over here." DeYonte stressed.

"That ain't even what I'm talking about but hurry up and kiss me." Peaches said,
DeYonte leaned in and kissed her lips. Lips that she once enjoyed kissing tasted like bitter ashes. She'd had enough and pushed him out and shut the door. She locked it then turned around and cried with her hands covering her face. She felt disgusted and violated; something so precious was contaminated. Antonio walked down the stairs ready to eat. Confusion was written all over his face when he noticed nothing had been touched. He noticed Peaches leaning back up against the door crying. Swiftly he walked over to her wondering what the hell was going on. She

didn't want to talk; she just wanted to be held and indeed he did so. He kissed her forehead as she cried in his arms.

When You Need a Friend

***Monday – September 23rd, 2019 – 12:38pm – Roseville Michigan*.**

Tangie drove up East Gratiot Ave headed to the Chipotle restaurant to meet up with Peaches. Tangie was in a no nonsense type of mood and the crazy traffic wasn't making it no better. She was pissed because the driver in the car behind her was speeding extra fast behind her.

"Bitch, if you hit my muthafuckin car Ima get out and whoop yo muthafuckin ass, hoe! Now get the fuck off my ass, bitch!" Tangie said emphatically, looking in the rearview mirror.

"Damn girl what's going on?" Peaches asked, voice coming through Tangie's car speakers.

"This stupid bitch behind me about to get fucked up if she hit my damn car! Stupid bitch." Tangie replied.

Tangie mashed on the brakes for a quick second to make the dumb bitch behind her slow the hell down. Eventually Tangie arrived at her destination and rolled her window down. She pulled up into the entrance and leaned her head out the window and yelled ***Dumb Bitch*** as the lady behind her drove by.

"Girl, calm yo road rage having ass down" Peaches said.

"I am calm; I'm just on ten." Tangie said, pulling into a parking spot.

"Well Ima need you to bring it down to about a four and a half until further notice." Peaches replied, sitting at an outside table waiting in her sun hat and sunglasses.

"Girl, you part of the reason I'm like this. You sitting up here on some murder she wrote shit with the hat and sunglasses on. Got me leaving work early to make sure my girl safe." Tangie said, shutting the car off and getting out.

Peaches got up and gave Tangie a hug. "Hey boo, thank you for coming."

"Of course, you know I got your back. Plus I got that Thiyow on me." Tangie said, being funny.

"Thiyow? What is that, like some Thai food?" Peaches asked.

"No dummy, that's a slang name for a gun, like as in bang bang." Tangie replied, sarcastically.

"Tangie, Ima need you to stop being silly. This is serious." Peaches stressed.

"Oh so you need me to be serious, serious? My bad, so what's going on?" Tangie asked, pulling out a chair and sitting down.

Peaches looked around vigilantly as she sat down. "Well…last night I had the most-craziest shit happen to me for real."

"What, did somebody put their hands on you?" Tangie asked.

"No, but somebody was in my house." Peaches replied, sipping her Vernors and glancing at traffic.

"In your house?!" Tangie asked, animated.

"Girl, me and Antonio was upstairs; we had just finished getting it in. I come downstairs to heat us up some food and this nigga DeYonte in my house on chill mode talking about he needs to talk to me and telling me he loves me." Peaches expressed.

"What in the entire fuck?! DeYonte?! From the job?" Tangie asked, eyes wide.

"Girl yes." Peaches replied.

"Girl yo milkshake bringing all the psychos to the yard! What's really going on?" Tangie said, leaning forward in her chair.

"Oh somebody is soooo funny right now. Is you finish or is you done?" Peaches asked, being sarcastic and mimicking Birdman.

"Finished? Hell nall I'm just getting started." Tangie answered, being her silly self.

"Tangie, I'm for real now." Peaches pleaded.

"Girl I am too but okay let me be more serious. What was Antonio doing this whole time?" Tangie asked.

"He was upstairs about to come down. I'm up here asking this fool how he got in my house and he tells me he picked my lock." Peaches said.

"How did he even know where you lived?" Tangie asked.

"Ain't no telling, you can look folks up online or maybe he was able to get a hold of my job information from work. Or maybe his ass just followed me home before; all I know is I was shocked." Peaches replied.

"That shit is the true definition of fatal attraction." Tangie blown away at what Peaches was telling her.

"Yeah this shit is scary." Peaches replied.

"But wait, hasn't Antonio's nephew been living with yall as well or something like that?" Tangie recalled.

"Yeah, but he's been over his cousin's house for the last couple of weeks; giving Antonio a bit of a break." Peaches said, glancing at her phone.

"Damn ain't no telling what would've went down if he was there." Tangie replied.

"But wait, I told DeYonte to leave or I was calling the police. He told me if I called the police he was going to show Antonio our text messages." Peaches said, looking at the guy walking past that resembled DeYonte.

"Y'all text messages? What kind of messages?" Tangie asked, eyebrow raised.

Peaches gave her a look like ***For real nigga?*** and Tangie gave her a look right back like ***Hell yeah I'm for real nigga now answer the question.***

"It was an incriminating message." Peaches said.

"Incriminating? Let's cut to the chase. Did you and DeYonte fuck each other?" Tangie asked, bluntly.

"Yes, but it was during that week Antonio and I broke up." Peaches leaned back and exhaled.

"Oh okay you're good then. Y'all was broke up so it was fair game." Tangie replied, sitting back like it was nothing to worry about.

"Yeah, but Antonio called me out when I said I needed some space and said that's because I wanted to be with someone else and I told him I wouldn't." Peaches said, feeling a bit guilty.

"Damn girl then what happened after you told him to leave?" Tangie asked.

"He still wouldn't leave. I pleaded and told him I'd call him later and he told me he wasn't leaving unless I kissed him." Peaches said.

"Kiss him? Didn't you say you and Antonio just finished getting it in?" Tangie asked.

"Yes." Peaches answered.

"Did you swallow?" Tangie asked, curious face.

"Tangie, you all blunt and shit." Peaches retorted.

“It ain’t nothing to be ashamed of. I would swallow the Atlantic Ocean if it came out of my man’s penis. Now did you swallow or naw?” Tangie asked, tapping Peaches on the leg.

“Yes Tangie, I swallowed every last drop. You happy now?” Peaches replied, shaking her head.

“Daaammmnnnnn…. Now see there? And that’s why you don’t break in nobody house stalking folks. You might get some babies in your mouth lol. He pressed you for a kiss and got a kiss from the whole entire family.” Tangie said, being silly.

“I’m so glad you find this hilarious.” Peaches replied.

“Okay I’m done being silly. I know this is something you hate to be dealing with, but don’t worry you not in this alone. We gone get you out of this.” Tangie said, walking over and hugging her.

Malevolent

Tuesday – September 24th, 2019 - 2:17 a.m. – Southwest Detroit. Excel drove down Michigan Ave headed eastward. He was coming from the Pantheion strip club. He was supposed to had been meeting Desmond, Shawn and Tim up there but they never showed up. Excel called Desmond and got no answer; he was trying to get into something before he grabbed the boys from big momma house. Excel remembered he had Shawn's number from when he called him the other day. He pulled up Shawn's name and before he could hit dial Shawn was calling him.

"Wdup doh, nigga?" Excel asked.

"Slow motion my nigga, just seen you drive past me headed the other way." Shawn answered.

"Oh okay, where you headed?" Excel asked.

"Shit, I was coming to fuck with you at the Pantheion. But I guess it's over with huh?" Shawn asked.

"I don't think so, I think they still cranking up there." Excel answered, looking in his rearview mirror.

"Damn, all the bad bitches probably gone from out that muthafucka." Shawn said, hitting his blunt.

"I doubt it, wasn't shit but fine as bitches up in that muthafucka deep. What happened to yall niggas coming up there?" Excel asked.

"Shit man, I don't know what happened to Desmond. Me and Tim got to fucking around with a couple lil bitches over here in the southwest and shit. We left from over there trying to fuck with some more hoes." Shawn answered.

"Aye check this out while I was up at the club and shit I seen one of them niggas we wrecked last week at the Crazyhorse." Excel said.

"What the fuck? You think that nigga was following you or something?" Shawn asked.

"Aye, I don't know. I just happened to see that nigga grimming me as I was walking out. Oh well fuck em; I would've beat that nigga ass if he would've said a muthafuckin word to me." Excel answered.

"Aye just be careful and watch ya back homeboy." Shawn said.

"And I hit a lick for a couple grand at the casino before I hit the Pantheion and I'm off that Hen Dogg! Man I wish that nigga would've tried any muthafuckin thing." Excel expressed.

"I bet yo ass blew all that bread on them hoes up in there." Shawn said.

"Hell nall, but I did blow some of it though most definitely." Excel replied.

"Where you headed to anyway?" Shawn asked.

"Big momma house to pick up the boys." Excel answered, looking at the women driving in the car next to him.

"Don't she stay not too far from the strip club?" Shawn asked.

"Yeah over here on Tillman." Excel answered.

"Oh yeah I know where that's at, I've been over there. Just be careful my nigga." Shawn said.

"Oh yeah I'm good." Excel assured.

"Aight my nigga I'll holla at you." Shawn replied and hung up the phone.

Excel dialed his son's phone to tell him to be ready to go as soon as he pulled up. His son didn't answer so he called back again and he answered.

"Hello, hey Dad." James answered the phone.

"Aye, get ready, I'm headed that way right now to pick you up.

"Okay." James answered.

"And don't be messing around either. It's late, I don't feel like waiting outside for you to get your stuff together. So already have your stuff together so when I pull up all you gotta do is get in the car and we can go." Excel said, frankly.

"Okay Dad, I'll be ready. See you when you get here." James replied.

"OH WAIT, hey you still there?" Excel, swiftly getting his son's attention before he hung up.

"Yeah Dad?" James asked.

"Tell little Carlos to be ready too because I gotta drop him off tonight." Excel stated firmly.

"Okay Dad." James replied.

"And tell him I said don't be messing around. Hug whoever you gotta hug or whatever; just be ready to go soon as I pull up. I'll be there in five minutes; I'm just around the corner." Excel said.

"Okay Dad. See you when you get here." James responded and hung up.

Excel continued driving down Michigan Ave and shook his head as he looked at the dirty, trifling dope fiends standing out there trying to trick for money so they can buy drugs. He had a half a cup of Dussé sitting in the cup holder from earlier. He started sipping it as he drove pass 24th street, and 23rd street and made a left on Tillman street. It was dark on the block with just a couple street lights that were half ass working and a couple of houses that were livable. The second street he drove past a four-story abandoned building on the corner to the left that the neighborhood dope fiends inhabited and slept in at night. He pulled up just a couple of houses down from the corner on the right and parked in front of the house. He lightly beeped his horn trying not to disturb the neighbors too much. James and Carlos did exactly what he asked and came straight out shutting the front door behind them. As the boys came to the car Excel noticed in the rearview mirror a set of bright ass headlights approaching and lowered his cup. ***Damn I hope this aint the fucking police! I got these damn warrants for these damn traffic tickets; Fuck…*** His heart thumped a tad bit harder as he tried to stay calm and not look to suspicious. ***Hurry up and get in and make sure y'all put on y'all seatbelts too***. The car pulled up on the side just as Carlos was about to put on his seatbelt. Excel looked and all he saw was sparking flames and he heard multiple gunshots!!! Everybody in the car was getting hit mercilessly! The sound of glass shattering and bullets pinging through the doors was traumatizing. Excel was slumped over to the right as his car door opened up. All he could feel as he helplessly laid there bleeding were hands yanking on his legs and raiding his pockets. All the money was aggressively taken out of his pockets! His necklace was snatched off his neck and a couple of other items were taken. The assailant jumped back in the passenger seat as they sped the hell off.

RING THE ALARM!!

September 24th, 2019 – 4:06 a.m. He never knew death could taste so fuckin bitter till it French kissed him on the lips…bullets lodged in his lower stomach and right thigh burned and ached excruciatingly!! Slowly he faded in and out of consciousness barely looking at the paramedic lady whose words were partially kept his attention. ***Stay with me, stay with me. What is your name?!*** His eyelids fluttered as he tried to focus on the questions she was asking him. Flashes of what happened to him went through his mind.

"Sir, what is your name?" Nurse Angela Wilson asked trying to get him to stay conscious.

"…Carlos." Carlos uttered as his breathing palpitated.

"Great, okay Carlos how old are you?" Angela Wilson asked, shining the ophthalmoscope in his eyes.

"Twenty-six." Carlos answered, sort of overhearing the other two paramedics that were working on him.

"Do you know who the President is?" Angela Wilson asked, realizing that his heart rate was starting to elevate more.

With short quick breaths Carlos answered "Obama…I mean Trump."

He's bleeding through; hand me another four by four quick. Carlos heard one of the other paramedics say wondering what they meant by that. He started getting nervous and slightly hyperventilating. Then he heard the medic say ***Keep pressure on it.*** He looked to his right and saw a pile of bloody four by four gauze on the floor and blood everywhere. ***What the fuck! Oh my God!*** He really started breathing harder and started going into shock!!! ***Carlos, stay with me. Look at me; look at me, Carlos.*** He looked at the EKG monitor trying to make out what the reading meant. The tightening of the blood pressure cuff caught his attention! He glanced at the saline bag dangling from the I.V. pole pumping fluids back into his body. ***Carlos you're starting to panic; I need you to relax and focus on me. You gotta stay calm, Carlos; you have to.*** She knew the more he panicked the faster his heart would speed up causing more blood to pass through the wound rapidly. She also knew that him seeing what was going on and him panicking was starting to cause him to go into shock which could lead to coma or death. The chatter behind her started to intensify.

"Carlos, stay with me. Do you have any kids?" Nurse Angela Wilson asked, quickly glancing at his vitals!

"Where's my Uncle?" Carlos panicked, vaguely noticing the orange strap across his chest that helped secure him to the gurney.

"He's waiting for you, Carlos so you gotta stay with me and focus." Angela Wilson said seriously trying not to lose him!

"What do those numbers mean? Am I dying?" Carlos asked, starting to panic more.

"That is your heart rate, Carlos. This is why we need you to relax; your uncle needs you to relax as well. Stay with me, Carlos." Nurse Angela Wilson answered.

The accelerated beep of the EKG monitor sounded traumatic to Carlos. His heart started beating faster and he became more nervous; he didn't want to die! He started fading out of consciousness. ***He's bleeding more; hand me two more four by fours! Keep pressure on the wound. Carlos stay with me! Carlos…Carlos! Stay with me. We're losing him…***

Life Goes On

6:47p.m. Antonio sat on his front porch stairs sipping a drink and gathering his thoughts. Life had just gotten a bit buck ass wild. He felt like he was reliving the hoodlum days of nineteen ninety-three all over again. He tried to logically think about everything that happened that night and backtrack. ***Who would gun down Excel and two young boys?*** His mind kept drifting back to the strip club where the drama jumped off just before it happened. He partially remembered what the dudes look like that went in the restroom and attacked Shawn. Everything seemed to have happened so fast on top of the fact they were intoxicated. He remembered as they were being put out the club the one dude saying ***Fuck you my nigga; believe me I'm gone holla at you my nigga. Trust me!! Ima holla at all you bitch niggas!*** Antonio was getting infuriated just thinking about that shit. Seemed like the devil was perched on his left shoulder urging him to go find that dude and kill him! He looked up and noticed Desmond and Niya pulling up and parking. Even though at times like this you may kind of want to be by yourself but it also feels good to have family and friends around to comfort you as well.

"Hey, hey what's up family?" Antonio asked after Desmond and Niya got out of the car.

"Hey, wdup cuz." Desmond asked, kind of sounding disheartened.

"Hey Tony." Niya said, shutting the car door behind her.

They walked up and Niya gave Antonio a hug.

"You okay." Niya asked sincerely.

"Yeah, I'm okay." Antonio replied with a partial smile.

"How is Peaches?" Niya asked, hating that they were all going through this drama.

"She was shook up earlier but she's better now; we went to go see nephew earlier and that kind of eased the stress." Antonio replied.

"Oh okay that's good to hear. Where's she at now?" Niya asked.

"I think she's in there making something to munch on now." Antonio answered.

"Oh okay, well Ima go in and help her." Niya replied.

"Okay that will be perfect." Antonio said as Niya headed on in.

Antonio shook Desmond's hand and hugged him.

"Wdup cuz?" Antonio asked.

Desmond exhaled with a face of frustration. "I'm cool, I guess."

"I feel you; I've just been out here thinking back about what the hell happened and who did this shit." Antonio said, sipping his drink.

"Sheeiit we know who the fuck did it. You remember what my man was talking at the strip club; talking about how he was gone holla at us. WORD TO GOD I got something for that nigga when I find him." Desmond said meaningfully, angered with a tightened jaw.

Antonio noticed Shawn pulling up and Timmy was in the car with him. They parked in front of the house next door and got out. They walked up not knowing exactly what to say to ease the grieving.

"Sorry what happened to your shorty and your cousins." Shawn said, giving Antonio some dap and hugged him.

"Thanks bro, I appreciate you for falling through."

Antonio replied, sipping his drink and gave Timmy some dap.

"How is Carlos doing anyway? I wanna go see little man if I can." Shawn asked as Timmy hugged Desmond.

"He cool, he cool, he took it like a soldier. The doctors said he should be straight." Antonio replied.

"Good, good. I just hate they smoked your cousin and his son though." Shawn replied.

"Yeah, that shit is fucking me up just thinking about it." Antonio replied, rubbing his face in slight frustration.

"Yeah man, I hate y'all going through this shit man. Hell, all this shit fucking me up to." Shawn said and then looked over at Desmond.

"Yeah, that shit just hit close to home." Timmy said, shaking his head.

"How the hell you holding up my dude?" Shawn asked Desmond, giving him dap and a hug.

Desmond just looked at him with a mean scowl on his face and gripping Shawn's hand tight as fuck. "Dog…I wanna kill these muthafuckas!"

"I know; look we gone handle that shit." Shawn replied sincerely, looking Desmond directly in the eye.

"Nigga, I'm so serious bro; I got too much shit happening, dog. I want these niggas dead violently! I'm going back to the old me." Desmond uttered passionately.

"Look my niggas, check this out. I talked to Ex just before that shit happened. He told me that he was at the Pantheon waiting on us and he saw them niggas we fucked up at the Crazyhorse last week. I think them niggas was following him." Shawn said.

"What the fuck, for real? Dog I know Im bout to bomb on these niggas!" Antonio said, furiously.

"My guy up at the club told me them dudes always up there. He also told me he should be able to get their whereabouts real soon. So we definitely gone holla at them niggas I promise you. Just give me some time and it's gone be open season on them niggas. You feel me?" Shawn asked.

"Bet." Antonio replied.

Desmond looked at Shawn and took a deep breath with an angered face. "Make that shit happen then."

Inside the house the ladies were trying to get things together. They were expecting some of the family to come over so she was preparing quick finger food for folks to munch on. Peaches had some deep stuff on her mind and was confiding in Niya. Niya could tell Peaches was going through it and stressing over her situation with DeYonte from her job. Niya fixed Peaches a drink and gave it to her.

"Girl what is going on? Is that dude at your job still stalking you after you told him to stop calling you?" Niya stopped and asked.

"Niya, he is wrecking my nerves and my brain. I had them move me to another department just so I don't have to see him and deal with him up close and personal. I'm also considering relocating to one of their other branches, and for the time being I took a week vacation to get my mind right." Peaches said, leaning back on the counter with her arms folded and drink in hand.

"Oh my God this is like one of them love, stalker, drama movies. Please tell me he dont know where you stay, Peaches?" Niya asked.

"Girl, this nigga showed up at my house the other day." Peaches said, looking around trying not to talk to loud.

"At your house?!" Niya replied, absolutely mind blown.

"Shhhhh girl don't be so loud! Antonio don't know!" Peaches whispered emphatically.

"Oh my bad, that's just some crazy sounding shit." Niya replied, looking around trying to be inconspicuous.

"And on top of that not only was he here but he was in here." Peaches said.

"In where?! Inside your house?!" Niya asked, eyes bucked.

"NIYA, you too loud." Peaches looked at her incredulously.

"I'm sorry my bad, but you telling me this crazy dude was in your house?" Niya asked.

"Yes, the nigga was in here." Peaches replied.

"Did you call the police?" Niya asked.

"He threatened to show Antonio our text messages if I decided to call the police, plus I just wanted him to leave. I didn't want anything blowing me and Antonio's engagement. I don't want to lose my man this time." Peaches said, looking down at her phone to see who was calling.

"Peaches you probably gonna have to come on out with the truth to Antonio because this shit is getting out of control. Next thing you know he'll be trying to eat breakfast with y'all; this can turn dangerous." Niya replied, noticing Peaches unpleasant look on her face as she looked at her phone.

Stress was the undeniable look on Peaches face when she looked at her phone and noticed it was DeYonte calling. Peaches sent the call to voicemail and immediately he called again. She didn't want to go to Antonio because how would she explain her and DeYonte's sexual encounter just days after they broke up? She got pissed, answered the phone and went straight at him.

"What do you want DeYonte? I told you I'm engaged!" Peaches said, listening closely to hear if the fellas were coming in the house. Her heart was pounding nervously.

"I need to talk to you; it's important." DeYonte answered.

"What is there to talk about? What is it?" Peaches sounded very irritable.

"I need to talk to you in person." DeYonte answered.

"LOOK, there is nothing for us to talk about; I'm engaged and that's that!" Peaches said, growing enraged and trying her best not to get loud!

"Peaches please stop doing me like this! I really need to talk with you. Plus I love you." DeYonte pleaded just as Peaches hung up the phone on him.

She then went in her phone settings and blocked his number....

Peaches and Niya speechlessly looked at each other thinking ***damn this shit has really gotten serious and has to stop before someone gets hurt...***

Get Well

Later on that night – 9:19pm Antonio and Desmond were up at the hospital visiting Carlos Jr. Carlos was sleeping and the fellas didn't want to just wake him up. Peaches stayed home getting some rest because she was exhausted. Niya also stayed home trying to get some rest and get her thoughts together. Antonio and Desmond were talking quietly as they watched the sports segment of the news on television mounted in the upper corner of the room. They were showing highlights of Blake Griffin, Andre Drummond and Reggie Jackson under Coach Casey. They noticed Carlos starting to move a little bit and saw that he was slowly waking up. Antonio hated seeing Carlos like this; it infuriated him as he looked at the I.V stuck in his arm, but he calmed and kept a cool head. Antonio got up out of his chair and went and stood at the side of the bed calmly looking down over him. Desmond was sitting in the chair at the foot of the bed, glad to know Carlos was doing a little better. There was a tray of food that Carlos finished a couple hours ago that was pushed over to the side. Carlos laid there in a little pain as he managed to talk with his Uncle and Cousin.

"Hey wsup young fella you've been sleep this whole time we've been back up here. We didn't want to wake you; we knew you needed the rest. The doctors are going to have to come in here shortly and check on you." Antonio said, hating to see him like that but glad he was getting better.

"I'm cool Uncle Tony, I'm glad y'all here." Carlos Jr. said, wincing as he slightly adjusted himself in the bed.

"You sure?" Antonio asked.

"Yeah I'm cool, Unc." Carlos Jr answered.

Carlos looked at Desmond "Hey wsup big cuz?"

"Nothing much Lil Cuz. How you feeling; are you feeling a lot of pain or just a little?" Desmond asked.

"Um I feel a little pain here and there, but it has gotten better." Carlos Jr. answered.

"Good, I'm damn glad to hear that." Desmond answered, peeping at the nurse with the nice ass that just walked past the room.

"Aye, if you feel up to it, I have a few questions I wanna ask you about that night this happened." Antonio said.

"No problem." Carlos replied, trying to recall how it played out.

"Were you able to see the face of the person who shot you?"

"Naw....um it was like everything happened so unexpected and fast the only thing I was really thinking about was trying not to get hit." Carlos Jr. replied, hating he couldn't actually recall who did it.

"It's all good, don't worry about it, we'll get to the bottom of this. The most important thing right now is that you're alive; that's all that matters." Antonio assured.

"Yeah lil cousin don't sweat it; you just get well. We gone find out who did this, trust me." Desmond added.

"I know, I know, I hate that I don't have any more details because I want to get to the bottom of this too. I just can't believe my cousins are dead. I wish I had a gun I would've." Carlos expressed with a tight face just as Antonio abruptly stopped him.

"Do not speak like that! You see what the street life can do to you and y'all wasn't even doing shit to nobody. That's not a direction I want you headed in and you know that." Antonio expressed.

"Yeah but" Carlos replied, yet abruptly interrupted again.

"Yeah but nothing, Carlos…I lost my mother due to gun fire. I lost my ONLY brother who was your father to the same type of violence that tried to take you out. Do you think I want to just allow something like that to happen to you? Do you?!" Antonio asked, slightly raising his voice.

"…no Unc, my bad, I apologize." Carlos Jr. replied, looking down.

"Look man…I'm sorry for raising my voice. My heart can't take no more losses like that. I mean you're the only thing I have left of my brother so I protect you at all cost." Antonio expressed sympathetically.

"I understand, again I apologize." Carlos Jr. responded humbly.

"You're all good Nephew; just get some rest. Me and Cuz are going to get up out of here and head home. We'll be back tomorrow to see you and see what the doctors say." Antonio said, extending his hand to fist bump.

"Okay Unc." Carlos Jr. replied, giving a meaningful fist bump to his uncle.

"Aye…make sure you always stay strong okay?" Antonio asked, deep and sincere.

"Okay Unc. You alright?" Carlos Jr asked.

"Yeah, yeah I'm cool; just a lot on my mind that's all." Antonio replied.

Desmond hated to see his Lil Cousin laid up in a hospital bed like this. He was angry about what happened but maintained his composure. He got up out of his chair and walked over to the side of Carlos's bed.

"Take it easy and get well Lil Cuz. Don't worry about a thang; we gone find out who it was." Desmond assured with a straight face and revenge in his heart.

"Thank you Big Cuz; that's why I love you." Carlos Jr. replied.

"I love you too Lil Cuz; stay strong and get some rest, man." Desmond said, fist bumping with Carlos.

Antonio's phone rang and he noticed it was Peaches calling.

"Hold on for one second y'all; this Peaches calling." Antonio said, stepping out into the hallway.

Overwhelmed

Tuesday – September 24th, 2019 – 9:37pm – Home. Peaches was relaxing in her T-shirt and panties, sitting in her bed sipping wine and on her phone scrolling through social media. She wanted to block out all the drama that had been arising in her life. Her eyes cringed at the ridiculous post she was reading and shook her head. She scrolled through a few comments and left one of her own. She read more comments and shook her head ***Muthafuckas just be saying any ole dumb shit on social media.*** She sipped her wine as she continued scrolling through her feed. A friend request popped up on her screen and she clicked on it. She clicked on the persons profile and clicked on photos ***Damn this nigga fine.*** After swiping through about ten or more photos she clicked on the friends list to see what mutual friends they have in common. However she wasn't fazed; she glanced at her engagement ring and smiled. Suddenly she thought about Antonio being up at the hospital visiting Carlos and decided to call him. She put the phone to her ear and figured she'd cook him something to eat in a moment.

"Hey babe, how is everything going up there?" Peaches asked.

"It's okay…" Antonio answered.

"Is everything okay? You sounding kind of dry." Peaches said, getting up off the couch and headed to the fridge.

"Yeah everything alright; little man good. He just in a little pain." Antonio replied.

"Okay tell him I love him." Peaches said, not noticing a masked man standing in the darkness of her dining room.

"Okay I will." Antonio replied.

"Babe, you sure you're okay." Peaches asked, opening up the fridge to see what all she was about to cook.

"Yeah, yeah I'm cool." Antonio replied.

"Well I'm about to cook, so you'll be able to eat once you get here." Peaches said, pulling out a pack of chicken thighs and sitting them on the counter.

"Okay great." Antonio replied.

"Oh and tell Desmond Niya been trying to call him." Peaches said, thinking she heard something by the side door.

"Okay." Antonio said, walking back in the room.

"Okay well, I guess I'll see you when you get here." Peaches said.

"Okay, see you when I get there." Antonio replied.

"Oh hey, I forgot to ask. Do you think yall going on strike?

"Hell I hope not, but it all depends on what GM and Ford do. They negotiate before us." Antonio answered.

"I'm sure everything will be okay." Peaches encouraged.

"Thank you." Antonio replied.

"Tony…I love you." Peaches said.

Antonio paused and said "I love you too Peachy."

"Alright bye sweetie." Peaches said, hanging up.

She sat the phone down on the counter and peered through the blinds over the kitchen sink. She looked around for a good second but didn't see anything. She noticed in the reflection of her neighbor's side window that the screen door on the side of the house was slightly ajar. She shook her head and went to go shut it. ***Ooohhhh I am going to get his butt for leaving this side door open like this.*** When she made it to the end of the hallway leading to the living room she looked to her left down on the landing where the side door was. She was briefly stunned and consumed with fright. She locked eyes with a masked man who was standing inside of the house in a red jacket looking at her. ***Oh my God*** immediately she darted the other way towards the back door. He chased her quickly ***come here bitch.*** To her surprise the other masked man was running up on her and grabbed her! She screamed as she tried to fight him off her ***let me go!*** She punched and clawed at him managing to scratch the shit out of his neck. The one behind her grabbed her around her waist picked her up. She cried, screamed and kicked the one in front of her in the nuts hard as ever. He got pissed and punched her in the face like a man and knocked her out cold....

RUDE AWAKENING

Wednesday, September 25th, 2019 - 3:47 a.m. Niya laid naked across Desmond's chest, both very lightly snoring. Desmond's cell phone rang but it wasn't loud enough to awaken either one of them. Whoever it was hung up and immediately called right back. Niya flinched a tad bit but neither one of them woke up. With all the things happening the last few days had everybody exhausted. Whoever it was hung up and immediately called back again. Niya winced as she raised her head and looked around and it dawned on her that the phone was ringing. She put her hand on his stomach and shook him ***Baby…baby…wake up***. Desmond slowly sighed with a scrunchy face ***What? What? Wsup bae?…*** Desmond was trying to figure out what was going on and noticed Niya was saying something to him. ***Baby, your phone is ringing and it's almost four in the morning. What if it's the hospital calling about Carlos or something?*** Desmond's phone rang once again so he reached for his phone. His heart slightly thumped as he thought to himself ***Please don't let no more shit be wrong***. Desmond nudged Niya ***Baby let me sit up for a sec.*** Desmond raised up and grabbed his phone; he realized that it was Antonio calling. He grew a bit nervous wondering what was going on. It had to be something serious if Antonio was calling like that. So he answered ***Yo, wsup Cuz, what's going on?***

"Aye man, Peaches is not here, dog and she ain't answering her phone when I call!! Ask Niya if she talked to her for me!" Antonio asked sounding seriously erratic.

"Wait, what?!" Desmond asked with a shocking look on his face.

"Man I swear to God I'm about to kill a muthafucka man!" Antonio yelled into the phone!

"Okay hold up Cuz, calm down so I can understand you, Bro." Desmond replied, cutting on the lamp next to the bed.

Niya was scared from the tone of the conversation and asked. "Baby what's wrong?"

"Ask Niya if she knows where Peaches could be or if she talked to her." Antonio asked Desmond to do.

Desmond looked at Niya "Antonio doesn't know where Peaches at. He asked if you knew where she was or if you've talked to her."

"What?! Nall, I ain't talked to her since we all left each other earlier. Oh my God! Ask him if he made a police report." Niya suggested, breathing heavily and frantically looking on the dresser for her cellphone.

"Tell her yeah I called to make a police report but they said it had to be twenty-four hours before you can file a missing person police report." Antonio replied, overhearing Niya through the phone.

"Oh yeah that's right, I forgot they want you to wait twenty-four hours before reporting it if someone's missing." Desmond recalled, getting up out of the bed.

"That is the stupidest fucking law! Anything can happen to somebody in twenty-four damn hours." Niya said, pissed. She tried dialing Peaches cellphone several times and was getting no answer.

"Okay I need to get me some cold water and get my thoughts clear. So look, okay wait a minute, did you talk to her earlier before we went to the hospital or the bar?" Desmond asked as he headed downstairs to the kitchen.

"I talked to her before we went into the hospital and let her know we were there. Then I texted her and let her know we were going to the bar to have a couple of drinks. When I got home the door was partially opened so I figured she just forgot to close the door when she came in the house or something. When I walked in everything was quiet and I'm trippin because I just knew she hadn't went to sleep and left the house open like that. After looking around the house and I didn't see her I called her several times and she didn't answer nor did she respond to any of my text messages. Now mind you, her car is parked in front of mine in the driveway." Antonio elaborated.

"Damn man, what the fuck? I mean I hate to ask this but…do you think she's out there fucking around with some dude?" Desmond asked, grabbing a bottled water from out of the refrigerator and leaned back up against the kitchen counter.

Antonio just breathed for a second and then replied "Man I don't know, dog. I ain't gone lie, the one thing that keeps going through my head is that nigga voice the other night."

"What nigga?" Desmond asked.

Niya's heart thumped hard as fuck the more she listened to the conversation.

"That nigga back at the strip club the other night. You heard what that nigga said. He basically said I know how to find y'all niggas; Ima come holla at you. I think them niggas went and popped Excel, his son, and Lil Carlos, and…" Antonio answered.

"And what? You think them niggas came and snatched her up or something?" Desmond asked as Niya looked at him with a really bad feeling in her heart.

"Man…I don't know Cuz…I just hope it ain't that." Antonio replied.

"What about this? You think maybe she could be over one of her girl's house drunk and passed out or something?" Desmond asked.

"I hear you Cuz, but nall she don't do shit like this. She don't even like getting drunk to the point she don't know what's going on; let alone leaving the house just open like this. This shit is just crazy man; flat out!" Antonio shouted at the end out of frustration.

"Okay Cuz look, you got to try to calm down so we can rationally think things through. That's the only way we're going to get a clear understanding of what's going on here." Desmond suggested, sipping his water.

Antonio exhaled and then replied "Alright dog, Ima try to remain as rational as possible…but I hope you're right…"

"Trust me, I am." Desmond assured.

There was a brief silence on the phone for a couple of seconds.

"Aye…I hope so…I don't want to have to go out here and kill one of these niggas tonight…" Antonio uttered.

"Cuz, can you please chill Bro; don't go doing anything crazy. We at least gotta find out what's going on before anything gets done. So look give it a few hours; try to get some shut eye and if she's not there when you wake up then me and Niya will be over there. Can you do that for me?" Desmond asked.

"Yup, I'll try." Antonio answered.

"Alright, holla back." Desmond replied.

His phone screen lit up signifying Antonio had hung up. He stood there and exhaled; he was just mentally lost. Niya walked back into the kitchen and sat her phone down on the counter. Desmond looked over at her with exhaustion written all over his face.

"Any luck?" Desmond opened up the cabinet doors and grabbed two short glasses.

"Well…I don't know…" Niya answered with a puzzled look on her face.

Desmond's eyebrows crinkled in the center, and confusion written in his face. He was curious about Niya's reply. "What you mean you don't know?" He grabbed the bottle of Moscato out of the refrigerator.

"Well…I don't even know where to start." Niya walked over and leaned up against the counter.

"Well you can always start with whatever you know. So, I'm listening…" Desmond replied, pouring them both a drink, and handing her one.

She took a nice sip of her drink. "I just tried calling her a few times and it would ring and go to her voicemail. I called again and it went directly to her voicemail."

"Sound to me like she possibly turned her phone off. You think she's out there fucking with another dude?" Desmond asked, looking slightly shocked and disgusted.

Niya just looked at him and remained silent and then looked away and sipped her wine.

"Wow that is fucked up that she's out here blatantly in the wee hours of the morning fucking some other dude. I wonder how the fuck she gone come home and explain this shit to him. She better have a good fucking lie for this shit." Desmond said, downing the rest of his drink.

"I never said that she was cheating; you don't know that. Don't put words in my mouth." Niya replied.

"I never said you said anything…but body language speaks volumes, and you can't even comfortably look me in the eye right now. She probably told you not to say nothing and that's why you just got quiet on me." Desmond said, wanting Niya to be honest with him about this.

"Look, I'm not trying to get caught in their little love quarrel." Niya downed the rest of her drink and poured her another glass.

"Baby, I'm not trying to put you in anyone's relationship problems; this is about Antonio's...missing…wife. Now if you know that she's okay or something then tell me that way I can relax a little." Desmond asked.

"Baby, I don't know exactly what's going on either; all I'll be doing is speculating. Plus I don't want you going and telling Antonio what I said." Niya replied, not knowing if she should tell Desmond the little she knows.

"Look, I know you probably don't want to put her business out there on blast like that, but baby… this can be critical to her life if you don't know for sure." Desmond expressed, reading into her eyes that she wants to really say something and then she looks away.

Niya looked up at the ceiling and exhaled; she hates these types of situations. However this wasn't just any ole situation. This was uncharacteristic of Peaches. ***Peaches would've told me if she was still messing around with DeYonte and going to see him. Why wouldn't she say something to me?*** Niya shook her head and looked back at Desmond.

"Desmond…this stays between me and you?" Niya said, hoping she's making the right decision.

"Okay, tell me." Desmond, sipped his drink.

"She's being stalked." Niya spilled the beans and then looked at him.

Desmond was caught off guard and had an incredulous look on his face. "Stalked? Stalked by who?"

"Her Ex." Niya replied.

"Her Ex? Her Ex who?" Desmond asked with a slight strange face.

"I mean I don't know; I think his name is DeYonte or something" Niya hated to say.

"What the hell? You think whoever this dude is she's seeing is trying to kill her or something? We definitely gotta tell Antonio so he can find her if her life is in danger!" Desmond expressed adamantly.

"Think about this; her phone was ringing all this time and now all of a sudden it's going straight to voicemail. Doesn't that seem kind of odd?" Niya asked.

"You don't know what's going on; like you said you're speculating." Desmond expressed, rubbing his face.

"That's exactly my point, babe." Niya replied.

"Look…I'm going to sleep on this…but if she's not located by time we get up and talk to Antonio then you need to tell him something. I know you and her have a close bond and y'all tight and all but if her life is in danger then all that home girl shit is out the window." Desmond said, downing the rest of his drink.

"Okay babe that's cool, but will you just stop thinking negative?" Niya asked, feeling a slight irritation.

"Okay whatever you say being that you know more than I do. I'm about to go back to bed; goodnight." Desmond said and headed upstairs.

Before he left the kitchen he stopped and turned around to say one last thing.

"Sweetheart, I'm not a negative person, and I wish you wouldn't think that of me; I just think realistic. Positive and negative is a part of reality and it's not wise to speak one sided." Desmond calmly expressed.

"And sweetheart sometimes both sides are not needed." Niya replied respectfully sarcastic.

"Yeah well I'm not gone argue about it and I actually hope you're right. But in the event that you're not this will be on your conscious; not mine." Desmond said and headed for bed.

"Get some rest sweetheart; I love you." Niya replied, putting her hand over her eyes and shaking her head hoping that she's right.

Till The Cops Come Knocking

Friday, October 4th, 2019 Peaches nice brown ass was spread doggy style at the side of the bed. Arched up perfectly with the perfect dip in her lower back she gripped the bed sheets as some dude stuck his dick inside of her. He admired the way the moonlight spilled through the window on her body. The song ***Till The Cops Come Knocking*** by Maxwell mixed in with her passionate moans and made him want to bust a nut all up inside of her. She loved the way he gripped her shoulders and pulled her hair; the thought of it was fucking mind blowing. He turned her over on her back right there at the edge of the bed; it felt like he was trying to stuff two yards of dick in her vaginal walls. She loved his sexual domination and rugged aggression. His firm hand choked her as he fucked her harder with every stroke! ***Smack me*** she said; turned on by him manhandling her and indeed he did so. He made her get on her knees and he spanked her lips and face with his brick hard meaty dick. He placed his shiny dick head right at her lips; she turned her head with resistance. She loved sniffing his balls as he rubbed them on her face. She licked them with her thick tongue and passionately sucked his testicles. She licked up his shaft and engulfed his dick with her mouth with the head in her throat. Her condensation was profuse as he clutched her hair tightly and she stretched her mouth wide open. Saliva spilled from her lips as she gagged on as much dick for as long as she could. She looked at him with a kinky ass look on her face, spit on his dick and then licked it off. The shit felt so good he couldn't take it no more; it was his turn! He made her get back on the bed doggy style again spread her legs. He lustfully sniffed her ass, buried his face all up in her cheeks, French kissing her vaginal lips and massaging her insides with his tongue. She felt like she was going crazy from the fucking thought of him doing it and the feeling! She knew she was about to explode; it felt like she could cum, fart, and piss all on his ass at the same damn time! She grabbed his head and straddled his face as her beautiful libations began to flow all on his mouth; the feeling was euphoric. She turned over on her back and motioned for him to get on top of her. She grabbed his throbbing hard rod and placed the head in her wetness. He slid his manhood all the way inside her. He fucked the shit out of her making the headboard repeatedly knock, and knock, and knock against the wall. It was literally sounding like someone knocking at the front door. Suddenly… The entire moment started to fade as Antonio slowly started to awaken. The headboard knocking seemed so real until he realized it was someone knocking at his door in real life. He shook his head and sat up squinting and blinking his eyes. He got up, slipped some shorts on, a t-shirt and headed for the front door. ***Who the fuck knocking at my door like they the police? Oh it must be Desmond and Niya***. His eyes cringed once he noticed a police squad car in front of his house; wasn't no question it was the Cops Knocking. His heart trembled a little as he wondered what they were about to say. He glanced at the time on his watch, noticing that it was twelve-fourteen p.m. He unlocked and opened the iron storm door.

"Good morning officers, please tell me you have some good news." Antonio said, as he looked at their plain faces.

"Good afternoon; my name is Detective Melvin Price and this is detective Valencia Stevenson. Are you in any relation to Ms. Peaches Galloway?" Detective Melvin asked.

"Oh my God, what happened? Where is she?" Antonio asked, dramatically.

"First can you please identify yourself sir?" Detective Melvin asked.

"Yes, I'm sorry; my name is Antonio Hunt; I'm her fiancé. I'm the one who called earlier this morning trying to make a missing person report. What's going on?" Antonio asked, feeling like it was getting harder for him to breathe.

"Unfortunately we're here to inform you that your fiancé was found dead earlier this morning." Detective Melvin said as calm as possible.

Antonio swallowed and paused for a second. He backed up and shook his head ***Mm mm, Naw Unuh, No, no, no, NO, NO, NO; y'all gotta have the wrong person! This gotta be a mistake.*** His eyes watered as he stepped back; a tear dripped down his face. ***Y'all wrong, right? Please tell me y'all wrong?*** Antonio shook his head, sat down on the floor and leaned back against the doorway leading to the living room. It felt like he was about to die as he stared around not knowing what to say. He couldn't believe that this was actually happening. Why couldn't this all just be a nightmare and go back to how it was? The detectives glanced around as they stepped inside. With her hand on his shoulder Detective Valencia bent down to talk to him.

"Mr. Hunt I know this is tough right now but we need to ask you a few questions in order for us to find out what happen if that's okay with you." Detective Valencia asked and Antonio nodded his head yes.

Valencia took her pocket note pad and pen out to jot down his information.

"Okay can you state your full name for me?"

"Antonio Darius Hunt." Antonio replied.

"How old are you?"

"Forty-two." Antonio answered, wiping his face.

"Date of birth?"

"November fifteenth, nineteen seventy-seven."

"Oh you have a birthday coming up." Valencia said.

"Yeah, but it won't even matter." Antonio answered, exhaled and looked at the ceiling in disbelief.

"And when was the last time that you saw her?" Valencia asked.

"Yesterday when I dropped her off at home right before I went to the hospital to visit my nephew who was shot days ago." Antonio answered.

"Do you remember around what time?" Valencia glanced at him and then back at her pad.

"Mmmm somewhere like around… eight p.m-ish." Antonio winced, guessing what time.

"Have you and Ms. Peaches ever had a history of domestic violence?" Detective Valencia asked.

"My fiancé was my best friend and my better half; I could never harm her." Antonio answered.

"Well I guess that's enough questions for now; thank you." Detective Valencia, putting her notes in her upper left pocket.

"Mr. Hunt, would you mind coming down to the station with us to help us further the investigation?" Detective Melvin asked.

Antonio nodded his head. "No I don't mind."

"We can drive you or you can follow us in your car; whatever's comfortable for you." Detective Melvin offered.

"I don't mind driving." Antonio replied as Detective Melvin offered him a hand and helped him up off the floor.

"Thank you." Antonio said, for being helped up.

"No problem." Detective Melvin replied.

"Just give me a hot second to put on some clothes and grab my keys and I'll be right out. Hey wait, are you thinking I did it?" Antonio asked very curiously.

"No, no this is just standard procedure. We just want to ask you questions and get your answerers on the record." Detective Melvin answered.

"Oh okay; no problem; I'll be right out." Antonio replied.

The detectives stepped outside and went and sat in the squad car.

Detective Melvin looked over at Valencia. "Well what do you think?"

Detective Valencia exhaled and replied. "Well he seems like a mild-mannered person. We'll need to find out if he knows if his fiancé had problems with anyone that would want to kill her. Did she owe anyone money? Was she involved with an ex-lover? Etc."

Detective Melvin recalled the crime scene. "I want to get a DNA check on that cigar we found beside her. Find out if any of her immediate relatives knows of any problems she may have had with anyone. She didn't just murder herself and I'm going to find out what happened."

"Absolutely." Detective Valencia replied with her eyes closed trying to put things together.

Antonio walked out the house; locking the door and shutting it behind him. He went and got in his car and followed the detectives for about ten minutes to the precinct. After getting there they had him sit in a room by his self for about fifteen minutes. The room was cold and lifeless; just a table and two chairs in it. Antonio glanced at the time on his watch and started wondering what was taking them so long. After a couple of minutes the detectives finally came in the room. Detective Valencia sat down in the other chair across from him and pulled out her notes. Detective Melvin stood beside her and looked on.

"Okay, I'm going to try to make this as quick as possible because I know you probably want to get on with your day and I definitely want to get on with mines. I try to be fare with everyone and make sure they are fully aware of their rights; this is just standard procedure." Detective Melvin said.

"Okay." Antonio replied.

"You know because it protects you and it protects us, and it makes you aware of everything that's going on." Detective Melvin said.

"Okay." Antonio, leaned forward in his chair.

"First one is you have the right to remain silent. Do you know what that means?" Detective Melvin asked.

"Yes."

"That means anything you say can and will be held against you in a court of law." Detective Melvin stated.

"Okay."

"Second is you have the right to have an attorney present while you're being questioned. If you can not afford to hire an attorney one will be appointed to represent you at no cost."

"Okay." Antonio answered, glancing at Valencia as she jotted down things on her pad.

"You also have the right to stop answering questions at any time."

"Sure." Antonio replied.

"Do you understand those rights?" Detective Melvin asked.

"Yes." Antonio answered.

"And you're down here voluntarily, correct?" Detective Melvin asked.

"Wait, say what?" Antonio asked, making sure he wasn't getting caught up in some type of trick question.

"Saying you're down here voluntarily; meaning no one forced you to come down here." Detective Melvin described.

"Oh okay then yes." Antonio answered.

"Cool." Detective Melvin replied and cleared his throat.

"Okay I just want to go over a couple of questions with you again for the record. Can you please state your full name?" Detective Valencia asked.

"Antonio Darius Hunt." Antonio replied, trying to relax in that uncomfortable chair.

"How old are you?"

"Forty-two."

"Date of birth?"

"November fifteenth nineteen seventy-seven."

"And what is your relation to Peaches?"

"Fiancé."

"And when was the last time you saw your Fiancé?"

"Yesterday when I dropped her off at home and my cousin and I went to see my nephew at the Hospital."

"Do you know around what time? I just want to establish a timeline for the record." Valencia asked, still jotting notes.

"Somewhere like around eight p.m."

Detective Valencia glanced down at her notes. "Okay do you have any idea who would want to do this to your Fiancé? Did she owe anyone any money? Did she have any issues with anyone like relatives, an ex-lover, friends or co-workers? We need anything you can think of to get to the bottom of this case."

"No, she doesn't have any issues with anyone according to my knowledge. However, I do have my own speculation as of who it could've been I just can't actually prove it." Antonio added, sitting back in his chair recollecting on the chain of events.

"Okay tell us what you know." Detective Valencia replied as she and Detective Melvin paid very close attention to every detail.

Antonio took a deep breath and exhaled. "Okay I'm going to try and be as detailed as possible. Saturday before last me and a few of the fellas decided we were going to go over to the CrazyHorse Strip Club on Michigan not too far from ummm…Livernois. It couldn't have been no later than about ten p.m. matter of fact I'm about sure it was ten when we got there. After being there for a short while and having a few drinks, food and a couple of dances we noticed it was a group of dudes from across the room that kept watching us. We kind of brushed it off and kept enjoying ourselves. Not too long after that my partner got up and went to the restroom. Not even a minute later it was two dudes that walked into the restroom, and that's when me and my cousin got up and walked into the restroom to make sure things was straight."

Detective Valencia stopped him for a second; she didn't want to miss a crumb of information. "Okay wait, what are the full names of your partner and cousin that went into the restroom starting with the name of your partner that went in first?"

"Oh um Deshawn Miller, we just call him Shawn, and my cousin Bernard Hunt." Antonio answered.

"Okay thank you; go ahead." Detective Valencia replied.

"So moments later security came busting in the bathroom, and they pulled everybody up out of there. They separated us and that's when one of the dudes we was fighting shouted out he knew how to find us and he was going to holla at us. Security made them go out of the front door and sent us out the back door. Then this past Tuesday I found out that my other cousin who was with us at the strip club and part of the altercation went to go pick up his son and my nephew and they got shot up. My cousin and his son died; my nephew survived and that's who we went to go see in the hospital. Then I finally come home and I noticed my side door is partially open. I go in, didn't see my Fiancé and it was strange because she never leaves the door open like that. I called her name and she didn't answer so I looked around; no sign of her. I figured maybe she was out with one of her girls being that her car was still parked in the driveway. I called her cellphone several times and got no answer. At about four in the morning I called nine, one, one to report her missing and I was told I had to wait twenty-four hours to make a missing persons report. Next thing I know you two were waking me up from a bad dream when you were knocking on my front door." Antonio concluded, sitting back in his seat holding his head and exhaled.

"So you think the murder of your Fiancé and the incident with your cousins and nephew are in relation to the altercation you guys got into over at the CrazyHorse Strip Club a couple of Saturdays back?" Detective Valencia asked with a straight face trying to piece this all together.

"Yes." Antonio answered.

"And you said you heard this guy that was across the room who was staring at you say he knew how to find you and he was going to holla at you?" Detective Melvin asked with a curious look on his face.

"Yes." Antonio answered.

"And have you ever seen any of the other dudes that were involved in that altercation prior to that night?" Detective Melvin asked.

"No, not that I can recall." Antonio replied.

"And was there any sign of forced entry on the front door you entered when you got there?" Detective Melvin asked, trying to catch him up in a possible lie.

"Front door? I said I came in the side door." Antonio corrected him.

"Oh sorry about that. Well did you recall seeing any sign of forced entry on the side door when you first walked in the house?" Detective Melvin asked.

"Not that I recall, but truthfully I wasn't actually looking for any forced entry on the door when I first got there so it's kind of hard to say without me going back and looking at it. However the door seemed to still operate properly so my mind wasn't even thinking about that." Antonio added.

Detective Melvin looked over at Detective Valencia and back at Antonio. "Okay, um, give us a brief moment so me and my partner can go talk a few things over. We don't want to hold up the rest of your day; we just want to wrap this up and get you out of here as soon as possible."

"Great." Antonio replied, hoping they hurry the hell up.

"Okay, we'll be right back." Detective Melvin said he and Valencia exited the room.

When Life Hardens Your Heart

Later on about noon Antonio was driving around feeling lost and spaced out mentally. He tilted his brown Kangol hat to keep the sun out his eyes. Slightly out of his right mind he had an opened bottle of Hennessy laying on the passenger seat. His pistol was in the glove compartment fully loaded. Vigilantly he'd look around from left to right and check his rearview mirrors to make sure no police were in sight. A slight bitter face he made as he sipped his liquor straight with no chaser. His cellphone rang; he glanced and saw that it was Desmond calling; he sat his drink down in the holder and answered it.

"Yo, wsup Cousin?" Antonio answered, sounding like he needed an escape from this reality.

"Wdup man? Been trying to reach you all day and see how you were doing. We heard on the news what happen to Peaches so we over here feeling it to. How you holding up?" Desmond asked.

"Sippin, burning petro, strapped and killing time; can't get my mind right." Antonio answered then sipped his drink again.

"Cuz, you know you don't need to be out there riding like that brah. AND you strapped too? Come on na you know you asking for it." Desmond replied.

"Oh well, I don't know what to do man…I can't escape this shit." Antonio uttered with a tight snarl on his face, trying to hold back tears.

"Cuz, come holla at me now man. I can't have you out here in the streets like that, dog. You're an easy pluck for the police." Desmond suggested.

Antonio was stressing and was caught in the duality of wanting to be around his family and wanting to be alone. After a short pause he replied "Aight I'll be right through there."

"Okay, I'll see you when you get here." Desmond replied.

"Alright, bet." Antonio hung up the phone and put it on the charger.

He rode in silence as he sipped his drink, the haunting thoughts were inescapable. He thought about Peaches and her beautiful smile. His eyes watered though he wanted to hold back his tears. ***Why God? Why me?*** He wiped his eye as a tear streamed down his face. It hurts even worse when you want to cry but you can't because people consider crying weak if you're a man. He thought about the day he proposed to her and how good they felt making it official. He thought about the last time he saw Excel, and how they were all laughing together and having a great time the other week. Then he recalled clearly the last words of ole boy they got into it with at the CrazyHorse, and his promise of revenge. By this time he pulled up in front of Desmond's house and parked. He got out the car, walked up on the porch and knocked on the door. He turned around and leaned his back against the wall and just looked up at the sky. He shook his head and rubbed his face; hating that he can't shake this never-ending nightmare. Desmond opened the door and greeted him in.

"Peace bro, come on in." Desmond greeted, giving Antonio a pound as he stepped in the house.

"Shit man, just waiting for God to wake me up from this nightmare." Antonio answered, shutting the front door behind him.

"I know man, we gone help you through this. Do you want something to drink? All we got is bottled water and wine." Desmond said as they made their way into the kitchen.

"Um…I'll take some wine I guess." Antonio answered, leaning back up against the kitchen countertop.

Desmond grabbed the wine out of the refrigerator and also grabbed a wine glass off of the cabinet. Niya walked into the kitchen from out of the den with teary eyes. She walked up and greeted Antonio with a hug.

"I'm so sorry for your loss." Niya said, stepping back and wiping her face.

"Thank you, Cuz; all of this has been eating me up inside all day." Antonio replied with eyes still slightly pink from crying.

"It's been killing me too." Niya said, flicking the hair back out of her face.

"That makes three of us. You want some wine, baby?" Desmond asked.

"Yes please." Niya answered.

Desmond decided he'd have a little wine himself and grabbed two more wine glasses out of the cabinet. He poured them and himself a nice glass of wine; it was time to toast.

Desmond looked at Antonio. "You know you're not in this alone."

Niya, looked at Antonio. "You're sure not, we family, and we got you."

The reality in a situation like this is deep and often unexplainable. He wished he could just scream to the heavens and change the entire past and bring her back. His eyes watered a little as it took everything in him to hold back the tears. Antonio just dropped his head and shook it.

"Indeed cousin, just do your best to hang in there; we're your support system." Desmond assured.

"I'm trying yall…but this heavy feeling has been crushing me all day y'all..." Antonio raised his head, and lifted his glass. "Let's have a toast in memory of Peaches."

They all simultaneously toasted and downed their drinks in memory of a beloved one who will never be forgotten; but surely missed forever…Peaches.

When A Cold Dark Secret Comes To Light

Thursday –October 10th, 2019– Lester Morgans Town Homes – 4:15pm. It was another ordinary day in the life of a detective; the body count continues. Two police squad cars swiftly drive up East Warren St. They arrived at the townhomes and turned up inside the complex. They pulled around the sharp curve and around to the address. Inside was Officer Howard Jamison age thirty-nine and Cortney Seldon age thirty-one. They both got out and approached the house; Officer Patrick Levy parked just behind them and got out as well. They walked up to the door and knocked; a young girl answered. She was sniffling and wiping tears from her face as she welcomed them in. The Officers immediately sympathized with her yet regretfully had to ask her about her deceased father.

"Are you the young lady who made the nine-one-one call about a man being murdered?" Officer Lamont asked.

"Yes." Ashley answered.

"I'm Officer Howard Jamison, this here is Officer Cortney and this is Officer Patrick. What is your name?" Officer Howard asked.

"Ashley." Ashley answered.

"Do you mind showing us the victim?" Officer Howard asked.

"Yes." Ashley replied, and led them up the stairs.

It is always eerie to go view a dead body but that's a part of life and definitely business as usual for the Officers. More tears streamed down Ashley's face as they made it to the top of the staircase to the living room and pointed on the floor to the right. Officer Howard confirmed it was a murder scene and asked Officer Patrick to go take the yellow caution tape and block off the area. Officer Howard looked around and Officer Cortney took out her note pad and jotted down every detail. The victim lied there on his back with a pistol next to his right hand. He was shot through the right eye; blood spilled down the side of his face staining the floor. Officer Howard then followed procedure and radioed it in confirming that there was a murder to the detectives so that they would be dispatched to the scene. Just under fifteen minutes later detectives Melvin and Valencia pulled up to the scene. They got out and stepped up under the yellow caution tape; it was a few folks here and there standing around looking as the Officers approached the house. The door was already opened and the detectives saw Officer Cortney speaking to Ashley in the entrance foyer. The Officer greeted the detectives as they entered the house.

"Hey guys this is Ashley, and Ashley this is Detectives Melvin and Valencia. She's the young lady who made the nine-one-one call about her father." Officer Cortney greeted and introduced.

"Sorry about your loss sweetheart. I promise we are going to investigate this case and bring you the best closure as possible." Officer Howard said.

"Where's the body at?" Detective Melvin asked, looking at Officer Cortney.

"Upstairs on the floor soon as you get up the stairs." Officer Cortney answered.

"Do you mind if we take a look upstairs?" Detective Melvin asked, looking at Ashley.

"No I don't mind." Ashley answered, wiping her face.

"Okay." Detective Melvin said as he and Detective Valencia made their way up the stairs; trying not to trip over the broom that was awkwardly in the way.

Officer Howard greeted the detectives as they stepped up into the living room. He nodded his head *Detectives.* They stepped over to the body to have a closer look. Valencia took out her camera and started snapping pictures for evidence. Officer Howard uttered lightly ***Love ain't even that important*** and shook his head. She snapped a picture of his entire body on the floor next to the pistol. She snapped a close picture of his bloody face. The bullet entered just above the right eye socket. She glanced over at his right hand and snapped a picture of it and the pistol lying on the floor next to it. Detective Melvin had a stern straight face; something didn't sit right with him. He slightly tilted his head sideways as he zeroed in on the dusty micro fragments of what appeared to be glass around the victim's body. He reached in his pocket and pulled out some clear sanitary gloves and slipped them on.

"Unhuh, I see a big problem with this suicide scenario going on here." Detective Melvin said, stepping closer and kneeling down by the body.

"Yup, who shoots themselves in the front of the forehead to commit suicide? Normally it's in the temple area or under the chin." Valencia replied, snapping another close picture of the victim's face.

Detective Melvin reached in his pocket and took out a very small envelope. He grabbed a tiny shard of glass off of the floor and looked at it closely and then placed it inside the envelope. He noticed a tiny sliver of glass sticking out from under the victims shoulder. He looked at the vaguely shiny sprinkles of glass on the floor; it appeared that someone had swept around the body. He glanced back at the broom on the staircase. He asked Officer Howard to collect the broom for evidence. He wanted to see if there was any broken glass particles in the broom and if it matches the glass particles in the envelope. He then noticed the slight scrape marks on the floor as if a table was drug across the floor or something.

"I'm willing to bet that this is a double homicide. This scene has staged written all over it." Detective Melvin said, looking up at Detective Valencia.

Melvin stood up and looked around; there was a five foot high entertainment system with a fifty-two inch flat screen television. He noticed an X-Box on the shelf just below it with a few games on the side. He opened one of the drawers and fumbled through them, and found nothing related to the crime. He went through another drawer and noticed a note pad that the victim had written in. He looked at the writing and wondered if it matched the writing on the suicide note. He politely handed the notepad to Valencia and asked her to compare the writing and see what she thinks. He carefully looked at the cabinet for a moment and noticed a couple of photos off to the side of the victim playing basketball; he was going for a left handed dunk in one of the pictures.

"Hey Valencia, can you come here for a second?" Detective Melvin asked, grabbing the picture off of the cabinet.

"What you got?" Detective Valencia asked.

"Do you see what I see?" Detective Melvin asked, handing the picture to Valencia.

She looked at the picture carefully and then her eyebrows cringed.

"Mmmhmmm…I see a southpaw about to dunk the basketball. And if he's a left hander then why would he shoot his self with his right hand?" Detective Valencia intelligently asked.

"Exactly, and I bet you those scrape marks on the floor and those slivers of glass came from a broken table and whoever did it tried to clean it up." Detective Melvin said.

"This is definitely not a professional job." Valencia added.

Officer Howard walked up the stairs and got the detectives attention. "I just looked in the garbage and found a garbage bag full of broken glass in the garbage dumpster out front. I also found a bent table in the laundry room."

"Which pretty much explains the scrape marks and shattered glass on the floor. I ultimately feel this crime scene will lead us to the killer in this case and in Peaches case. We just need to wisely piece together all of this evidence till it spells out the name of who did this. We also have to retrieve that bag of glass from out of the garbage; I'm sure that it has some type of DNA on it from this case." Detective Melvin said.

"And to add a little clarity to the case; I asked the young girl if her Father was right-handed and she said he was left-handed." Officer Howard said as the detectives just looked at each other.

<u>*Precinct*</u>

Detective Valencia sat in her office slightly cluttered with paperwork going over the evidence; she and Detective Melvin were determined to crack this case. Her phone rang so she answered it; she immediately got up and walked to the fax machine and grabbed the documents that had just came through. She looked at it and walked swiftly to Detective Melvin's office. ***Thank you so much; I can't believe you got it back to us this fast. I owe you for this and ass is not a part of the deal. I'll call you later.*** She hung up the phone as she knocked on the door and Melvin told her to come in. She stepped inside and handed Detective Melvin the documents. He looked at them closely; it was regarding the DNA results for Peaches and DeYonte. He looked back up at Valencia ***Oh this guy who ran these DNA test must really like you to get them back to us this fast. I know exactly who to turn to when we need speedy DNA results.*** Detective Valencia just looked at his sarcastic ass, brushed his comment off and replied ***anyway, we got leads to go off of now.***

"Okay well looking at Peaches DNA fingernail swab results suspect number one is Timothy Johnson and suspect number two is Shawn Miller…this Shawn Miller dude looks familiar. And the DNA results yields Timothy Johnson as well; we have a common denominator we need to go pay a visit to." Detective Melvin said, sipping his coffee.

"Did you find out anything?" Valencia asked.

"Oh yes; I made a stop and talked to the optometrist and she said she believes this DeYonte and Peaches case was a double homicide. She said the scene looked staged to her; DeYonte's right forearm had a nice bruise on it indicating he was attacked and defending himself. She said the way the bone was fractured it would have been practically impossible for DeYonte to have fired the gun on himself with his right hand." Detective Melvin said, looking up at forensic specialist Jeff Weaver entering the office.

"Hey you guys I have some vital information about this Peaches and DeYonte case." Jeff said.

"The puzzle is coming together great; okay shoot it." Detective Melvin replied, eager to hear what he had to say.

"Well we do know the Peaches and DeYonte cases are related to the same source. Ballistics shows that the bullets that were retrieved from both victims were definitely fired from the same gun. Also we found fragments of red mulch in the footprints at both crime scenes." Jeff stated.

"Good, good, very good, thank you." Detective Melvin replied, tapping the desk with his index finger while processing all of this.

"I'm sorry; also we found out that this same gun was used in the murder of Mr. Bernard Hunt alias known as Excel as well as Bernard Hunt the third and the shooting of Carlos Hunt Jr." Jeff added.

Detective Melvin just shook his head and said "We gotta go bag these sorry bastards."

Man Hunt

The sound of the tires squealed as the raid van and squad cars turned the corner on Anglin Street. The engines roared vehemently as they rushed down towards the middle of the block. Neighbors who were outside looked on as police abruptly stopped in front of Timothy's house. Some people took out cellphones and started recording just any foul police shit jump off like it did in Fergusson and Baltimore. Cops immediately got out heavily armed with high powered weaponry. Some of them quickly made their way up on the porch and a few of the others made their way around the side of the house. They were positioned on both sides of the front door with guns in hand and fingers on the trigger. As soon as they got ready to knock on the door before smashing the door off of the hinges the door opened. Timothy had his back turned and was pulling the trash bag about to take the garbage out. Never did he see the police behind him.

"Timothy Johnson, put your hands up and don't move!!! Naw don't try to run, I said don't move!" Officer Howard yelled as police rushed Timothy.

They forced his chest up against the wall and cuffed his hands behind his back.

"What the fuck are y'all doing?! I ain't did shit to nobody!" Timothy said, pissed off because they were strong arming him.

"You're under arrest for the murders of Peaches and DeYonte." Officer Howard strongly replied.

"Da fuck is you talking about?! I ain't did shit to nobody?" Timothy replied, heart pounding and wrist irritated from the tight uncomfortable squeeze of the handcuffs.

"Oh yeah? Well save that shit for somebody that's stupid. Your DNA is all over those crime scenes." Detective Valencia said, as she noticed a black woman in her late forties walking into the living room trying to see what the hell was going on.

"What is going on? Where is Derrick?" The woman asked.

"Aye Gina, they arresting me for something I ain't even done!" Timothy responded, being tugged out of the front door.

INTERROGATION

It was business as usual at the police precinct. Officer Howard walked Timothy inside this small room with his hands still cuffed. ***Alright I need you to hold steady so I can take these cuffs off of you.*** Officer Howard took his keys and unlocked the cuffs. *Okay you can have a seat and the detectives will be right in to talk to you.* Timothy sat down in the hard ass metal chair in front of this small wooden desk. He looked up at the officer ***Aye man, can you bring me a water?*** The officer looked back at him and replied just before he shut the door ***I'll have the detectives bring it in when they come.*** Timothy looked around the cold little room; there was a surveillance camera mounted in the upper corner. He shook his head and leaned forward placing his elbows on the desktop with his hands covering his face. ***Fuck!*** He thought deeply on what he was going to say to the detectives when they questioned him. He thought long and hard on the situation; he shook his head helplessly in his palm. ***How the fuck did they pin this murder on me???*** Not too far long afterwards the door opened and Detective Melvin and Valencia walked in and shut the door behind them. Detective Melvin had a few items in his hand that he'd placed on the desk as well as a handheld voice recorder. Valencia handed Timothy a bottled water and stood back up against the wall; she didn't feel like sitting. Detective Melvin sat down in the other chair and pressed record.

"Can you state you name for the record?" Detect Melvin asked.

"Timothy Johnson." Timothy answered, sitting back and slouching in his seat.

"How old are you?" Detective Melvin asked, examining Timothy's body language.

"Thirty-six." Timothy answered.

"You do know why we have you here today asking you these questions?" Detective Melvin asked.

"I understand that I am being framed for a murder I never committed and know nothing of?" Timothy replied.

"Oh really? We're setting you up? Oh okay, well sir don't play with me. I'm trying to give you a chance to state your side of the story." Detective Melvin replied, looking at him with a serious face.

"Dude I told you I didn't kill nobody. I have no damn idea what you are talking about." Timothy replied, getting pissed.

"First of all sir calm down with all that; it's not gone help you at all." Detective Valencia said, not appreciating all of that anger and attitude.

"Well I ain't do it; y'all got the wrong guy." Timothy replied with a mean look on his face.

"Oh yeah? Well that ain't what your boy Shawn had to say about it. He said you did it." Detective Melvin said, using his skills to call Timothy's bluff.

Timothy was briefly stunned and caught off guard; he looked like a dear caught in headlights. His heart raced though he tried to keep his composure.

"You lying, Shawn ain't told you nothing like that. You can get out of here with that one." Timothy replied, trying his best to think of what to say.

Detective Melvin was one of the best in his field and he definitely knew his shit. He could tell by Timothy's lack of confidence, lack of eye contact, and demeanor that he was breaking him slowly. He just relied on the evidence that was retrieved and researched as well as his intelligence.

"Oh yeah, Timothy? How you think we know about your red jacket you were wearing that night and the pistol you shot Peaches with? It's easy to get a little bird to talk when their back is against the wall and he pinned this whole murder on you playboy." Detective Melvin said firmly, opening the large envelope that was on the table and pulling out an unloaded pistol and placed it on the table.

"The more you continue to lie the worse this is going to get for you. I promise you that you will never see the outside world again nor will you EVER enjoy life outside of these prison walls with your children again. Now MAYBE if you can tell us the exact truth then MAYBE we can lighten your sentence, but it all depends on what you have to say here today." Detective Valencia said convincingly.

"And just so you know we found your DNA under her fingernails; she must of scratched you really hard. Is that where that scratch came from on the side of your jaw right there?" Detective Melvin asked.

Timothy just looked off at one of the walls, closed his eyes, shook his head and sat there in silence.

"Timothy, we do not have all day. Now we're trying to help you, but you gotta be willing to help yourself." Detective Melvin stated, looking him dead in his eyes.

"Man.........I don't know what y'all talking about." Timothy said reluctantly, thinking how he wished he could kill Shawn.

"You know what? This is the last thing Ima say. I can care less if you ever see the light of day again because in the end Ima go home to my family. So let me say this.... You know that red mulch that was spilled all over your basement floor? It matches the same red mulch residue we found in the footprints at the scene of the crime...I'm going to let you let that one soak in for a minute." Detective Valencia added.

"Sounds like she got you by the balls there buddy. SO.... last chance to tell us exactly what happened. I want to know who all was involved, why was she murdered, I want to know every got damn single detail. I want to know WHO KILLED Peaches and DeYonte?" Detective Melvin demanded with a mien scowl on his face.

Disgust was written all over Timothy's face...he shook his head and looked away. Detective Melvin was growing impatient and was ready to call his bluff one more time. He could look in Timothy's eyes and see he couldn't believe he'd been ratted out. He just couldn't believe he had gotten played like that. Where was all of that loyalty at?!! But fuck that! He figured how else would they know about the color coat he was wearing. He also felt why the fuck should he remain silent and take the wrap for some bitch ass nigga who ratted him out... Detective Melvin decided to call his bluff one last time.

"Okay cool. Don't snitch, you got the rest of your entire life to reflect on your loyalty while you're locked in a cage till you die. So you just wait right here; an officer will be here shortly to escort you to your cell." Detective Melvin said as he started gathering the items he brought to the table.

Timothy knew basically he was fucked at this point. The detectives were walking out. Reality started kicking in and the thought of being enclosed in a nasty ass cell with a bunch of nasty ass niggas. It made him start questioning himself. ***Damn is not snitching even worth this***

shit especially after being ratted out. He wanted to cut whatever deal he could just to walk the street again one day. Just as Detective Melvin was about to close the door behind them Timothy hurried up and urgently got their attention!

"OKAY, okay, okay, wait a minute…come back in." Timothy asked though the thought of betrayal was convicting him.

The detectives stopped and looked at him to see if he was for real then came back in. They knew the entire time that they had never spoken with Shawn nor located his whereabouts, but at least they will have a statement against him when they find him. Detective Melvin eased back into his seat. He took out the recorder again, placed it on the deck and hit record. He looked at Timothy with a straight face.

"Here's your one shot to tell us everything you know and we'll work on getting you a lighter sentence…

Secrets Never Remain Silent

Friday October 11th, 2019 Desmond was driving home on his way from the supermarket; he had grabbed a few things for dinner. He was actually thinking about really starting this new chapter in his life. He wanted to take finishing his novel about his life more seriously and becoming a published author. His cellphone rang and he looked down at it and saw that it was Antonio. He answered the phone and put it on speaker since the police was just up ahead.

"Yo, wdup Cuz?" Desmond asked, slowing down and stopping after the bus stopped in front of him.

"I'm fucked up, Dez." Antonio answered, sounding really horrible.

"Fucked up? What happened?" Desmond answered, finally getting over from behind the bus and stopping at the red light.

"Dog…I don't even know where to start; I'm just totally fucked up…and I just want to tell you that I love you. Don't ever forget that." Antonio answered, sniffing.

"Dude, you're scaring me now. You over there crying?" Desmond asked with a curious face and driving after the light turned green.

"Nope." Antonio answered, sniffing again.

"Cuz, what the fuck is going on with you?" Desmond asked, now very concerned.

Desmond felt deep down Antonio was crying and was lying about it. Antonio sniffed again and there was a silent pause for about ten seconds.

"I can't go on like this…I don't want to live no more; I hate this life." Antonio answered.

"COUSIN, what the fuck is going on dog? You talking crazy right now. Hold up just calm down, I'm about to head your way. I'll bring some drinks and we can chop it up, cousin to cousin." Desmond said, accelerating through traffic after police turned at that last light.

Desmond's phone beeped and he looked and saw that it was Niya calling in. He asked Antonio to hold on real quick and answered the other line as he swiftly maneuvered through traffic.

"Hey Queen, I'm on the other line, got some serious drama going on. Wsup?" Desmond asked, wanting her to hurry up.

"Drama, what's going on?" Niya asked, thinking what more could actually be going on.

"Antonio just called me basically talking about killing himself; talking all this he don't want to live no more." Desmond answered, sounding frantic and distraught in thought.

"What the hell, are you serious?" Niya asked, totally shocked.

"I'm dead serious, babe. Let me call you back." Desmond said, trying to think of the fastest alternate route to Antonio's house since all of this road construction was going on throughout the city.

"Okay bae." Niya replied.

"Okay boo." Desmond said, and clicked back over to the other line.

By that time Antonio had hung up the phone so Desmond immediately called him back but got no answer.

Desmond called back a second time and again it rung and went to voicemail. Various thoughts were racing through Desmond's mind as he headed to Antonio's house. He wanted to think positive like people say but he didn't want to pretend like something wasn't wrong for the sake of being positive. He thought out loud ***Come on Cuz, don't do no dumb shit; just hold on till I get there.*** Desmond finally made it to Antonio's street and hurried up the block safely and fast as he could. He pulled up and parked in Antonio's driveway. He looked and saw the front door was opened; he hoped everything was okay. He got out the car, walked up on the porch and knocked on the door. Looking through the screen door he didn't see or hear Antonio at all. ***Yo Antonio, come open the door.*** He peered through the partially closed window blinds to see any movement and rang the doorbell; still no answer. He twisted the handle on the door and it was unlocked; this was so not like Antonio. He stepped inside and entered the quiet living room. ***Yo Antonio, where you at?*** He made his way to the left where the kitchen was and saw Antonio slumped over face down on the kitchen table. ***What the fuck? Antonio what up?*** Desmond was completely thrown the hell off and panicked when he noticed Antonio was faced down in a white powdery substance scattered on the table and a pistol next to his head. ***Oh my God is this nigga dead?*** Desmond walked over to him and shook him. ***Antonio...yo Antonio.*** He grabbed his shoulder and tugged on him slightly and Antonio finally came to. He winced as he slowly eased up off the table with a ugly, confused look on his face like he'd just awaken from a good ass nap. It looked like someone took a palm full of powder and slapped the shit out of him. Antonio had been snorting cocaine to literally escape reality; residue was all over his face.

"DOG, what the fuck, man? Cocaine Cuzzo, are you fuckin kidding me?" Desmond asked, blown away by this shit.

Antonio shook his head pitifully in shame and humiliation. He looked up at Desmond with a bleak stare, sounding very inebriated.

"It doesn't matter…it doesn't matter no more Dez, my life is done; I've accepted it."

"Yo, yo don't talk like that Cuz, we better than this. What do you mean your life is over?" Desmond asked, looking slightly disgusted.

"My life is what doesn't matter; it's all over now." Antonio said, chuckling.

"Antonio, I know you lost Peaches and I know Excel and little cuz got murdered, but cousin, life goes on. I'm not trying to sound insensitive but it's true." Desmond tore a piece of paper towel and told him to wipe his face.

"When a man has totally been destroyed mentally to the point of no turning back it's over." Antonio replied, half ass wiping his face and without thought let the paper towel fall to the floor.

"Man, I just need you to relax; I promise I will help you get through all of this." Desmond said, pulling out a chair and sitting down.

Antonio chuckled again; eyes barely able to stay open. "Thank you Dez…you've always been a real brother to me. I guess I have to be honest with you; it probably would've came out anyway so here it is…I killed Peaches."

"Oh hell to the nall, stop sniffing that shit; it has you talking delusional now." Desmond said, looking at incredulously.

"Dez, I'm serious." Antonio replied.

"Antonio, you were with me the night she got murdered. Snap out of this shit, dude!" Desmond said, getting frustrated.

Antonio managed to look at Desmond with a straight face and shook his head. He rubbed his finger through the coke on the table and sniffed it; the rush was intense. "Wheeeewww I never knew a high could feel this got damn good! Oh baby!" Antonio expressed animatedly.

Desmond stood up "Antonio look at me; that shit is killing you. It has you talking outrageous, man. I need to get you some help before that shit kills you."

"Kills me? Believe me this shit can't kill me no more than I already am. I'm a dead man walking on good ole death row, Cuzzo." Antonio replied.

"What?" Desmond asked, looking at him strange.

"Yes sir, the bitch sentenced me to death without ZERO chance for parole." Antonio expressed, peeking outside the window.

"What…are you talking about?" Desmond asked, looking at the believable look on Antonio's face looking back at him.

"Peaches Dez, I had Peaches killed. I planned this whole shit including you and I going to the bar and me paying for everything with my credit card. That way I was able to establish a paper trail and alibi to cover my ass." Antonio said, slightly nodding.

"Dude, you're for real aren't you?" Desmond asked, absolutely stunned.

"And you know who I had do it? Shawn and fuckin Timothy. Yup that's right I had our own fuckin friends kill my Fiancé. And I know how crazy this shit sounds and I bet you're thinking why would I kill my Fiancé and we just got engaged. Well let me tell you the bitch killed me first!" Antonio replied hysterically, chuckling as he closed his eyes.

"Man…I want you to get some help." Desmond replied, leaning back against the kitchen cabinet.

"Dude, I looked at Peaches computer one day after hearing one of the alerts go off and noticed her Facebook page was opened. Not expecting anything wrong I just looked at it and you know what I saw. I saw an inbox from a male coworker…" Antonio said.

"And what did it say?" Desmond asked.

Antonio paused for a second and said shamefully. "It was what I saw."

"What was it?" Desmond asked, hoping it wasn't what he thought he would say.

"Cuz, can you even fathom….your Fiancé receiving a video message from another dude… a video of your woman sticking another man's dick in her mouth?" Antonio asked.

"What the fuck, Bro?" Desmond replied.

"Dog, this nigga was fucking my woman, Bro…Nigga treating my Queen like his little hoe… And I'm supposed to just be normal after seeing that?" Antonio asked, sincerely.

"Damn dog, I really hate you had to even experience some shit like that." Desmond replied.

"Bro, that ain't all." Antonio said.

"There's more?" Desmond asked.

"Now this is really gonna blow you away. Hows about not only did this nigga send a video of him fucking my babe; but this nigga sent her a message screaming in all capital letters that he's been trying to call her phone, telling her how he loves her and that he has A.I.D.S. He said that he doesn't know if she gave it to him or he gave it to her. MY FIANCE Desmond…my Fiancé contracted

A.I.D.S. So I immediately went to the hospital and got tested and dammit I tested positive…I'm dying Dez…I'm dying." Antonio said, as his hand started to tremble nervously on the table as tears dripped down his face.

"Bro." Desmond said, absolutely flabbergasted.

"Aye, I asked her if she wanted to see someone else. I asked her about all that social media inbox bullshit. Now she really going to be in a box; a PINE BOX." Antonio said, emphatically.

Antonio leaned and peered through the small openings in the blinds. His hand slowly stopped trembling then he took a deep breath and swallowed. Desmond noticed Antonio's abrupt change of emotion and was curious. *What you looking at out there?* Desmond took his finger and slightly pulled down one of the blinds to see what was out there. The Police had pulled up in a raid van and a few squad cars and got out. Antonio looked at Desmond ***go open the door Cuzzo***. Desmond was straight stunned and felt absolute lost. ***This has nothing to do with you Desmond…what's going to happen is going to happen and you can't do nothing to stop it.*** The police swiftly approached the house high powered weaponry and got in position. Three officers stood on the front grass with guns pointed at the windows, the side of the house and one at the front door. Three officers ran up on the porch; one of them went to the side of the porch to help cover any violent activity coming from the side of the house. The other two officers opened the screen door and positioned themselves on both sides of the door with their hands on their rifles. The moment was geared to be intense as the officer knocked on the door a few times! *Okay* Desmond opened the door and put his hands up. The officer watched Desmond closely *Keep your hands up and step outside!* An officer quickly patted him down and before anything could happen a loud BANG went off in the house. Everything seemed surreal at that moment as Desmond watched the officers go in the house cautiously. Soon as they entered the kitchen they found Antonio lying on the floor dead. He had put the gun in his mouth and blew his own brains out; blood and brain matter stained the wall where he was sitting at in the chair.

When Truth Comes to Light

Later that evening Niya was at home in her kitchen preparing dinner. It had gotten very late, she hadn't heard from Desmond and started to worry. Carlos Jr. was in the guest room resting; gradually recovering. Stressfully she ran her fingers through her hair and sighed. She picked up her phone and dialed Desmond's number for about the forth time; unfortunately it didn't ring and went directly to voicemail again. *Come on Desmond what the fuck is going on?* With all the killing that's been happening close to home, Carlos Jr. getting shot, plus all of the police racially killing black men and getting away clean she couldn't help but worry somewhat. Her eyes watered as a tear dripped down her cheek. She had to move the pan off of the cooking eye that was lit because she didn't give a damn about cooking right then. Immediately she felt relieved when she heard keys jingling at the front door and the door opening. Between her being emotional, nervous, and happy she didn't even let Desmond get in the door good before she started talking.

"Oh my God Desmond, where have you been?! I've been calling you non-stop and going straight to your voicemail. What happened, where you been? I've been a fuckin nervous wreck." Niya expressed emotionally hyper and nervous.

"Baby calm down, you can't even get your words out right because you're talking so fast." Desmond said as he shut the front door behind him.

"I know, I know, but you know how I get when I'm nervous." Niya replied, slowly calming herself down.

"Well, my phone battery died and I had no charger to charge it up. I've been at the police station all day being questioned like they were interrogating a terrorist." Desmond replied, leaning up against the kitchen counter exhaustedly.

"The police station? What the hell happened? Where is Antonio?" Niya asked, nervous about what she thought Desmond's answer would be.

Desmond shook his head and looked at the floor and took a pause… "Antonio's dead, babe."

It felt like Niya's heart dropped through her stomach as she stood there stunned with her mouth slightly opened. She felt hollow and helpless; wishing she didn't hear what Desmond just told her and she could just wake up and all of this never happened. She more so felt for Desmond because that was his blood Cousin so she walked up to him and hugged him compassionately.

"I'm so sorry, King." Niya said.

"It's okay, Queen, and thank you." Desmond replied, hugging Niya back.

"What exactly happened?" Niya asked, looking up at Desmond.

Desmond sighed, took a step back and asked Niya to have a seat as he sat down himself at the kitchen table. Niya's heart thumped as she sat down.

"After I hung up with you to click back over to the other line to finish talking with Antonio he had already hung up. I called him back a couple of times and he never answered. I got scared hoping he hadn't killed himself. I flew over there as fast as I could and whipped up at his house. I walked up on the porch and rang the doorbell but he never came to the door. I just so happened to fuck around and twist the door knob and the door was unlocked. I walked in and found him slumped over on the kitchen table. His face was laying in cocaine and he had a pistol lying next to his head." Desmond said, interrupted by Niya.

"Cocaine?! What the hell?!" Niya asked, blown away by what she was hearing.

"Yes, cocaine, but wait a minute just listen to the rest; it gets crazier. I called his name and eventually he sat up and got all of this cocaine all over his face. Eventually I got him to talk to me and he started telling me about one day he found this email this guy had sent to Peaches. Obviously it was some dude Peaches had been fucking around with because the dude in the email said he gave her A.I.D.S or vice versa. Antonio said at that point he went and got tested and it was confirmed that he did have A.I.D.S. He said from that point he paid Shawn and Timothy to kill her and the guy she was involved with. Then the next thing you know the police ended up pulling up; Antonio told me to go let them in. I was actually stuck for a moment not knowing what to do especially with all these trigger happy police killings us out here. By the time I reached for the door to open it the police had burst the door open, had guns in my face and told me to put my hands up. About two seconds later a gunshot went off in the kitchen; Antonio blew his own fuckin head off. Police took me down to the precinct, questioned me and here I go." Desmond expressed.

Niya was absolutely flabbergasted with her eyes wide with shock and disbelief.

"Oh my God, it all adds up now." Niya replied, slowly shaking her head.

"What are you talking about? What adds up?" Desmond asked, looking puzzled.

"Ole boy that they killed was the dude Peaches was trying to get rid of. She didn't want no drama especially since she was getting married. He was calling her like crazy so she blocked his number and I bet you that's why he sent her that email. I mean it's all kinda clicking to me and making sense. They just talked about it on the news not too long ago. They were saying how detectives investigated and ballistics revealed that the same shooter that killed Peaches and DeYonte was the same shooter who killed Excel and shot little Carlos that night." Niya replied, shaking her head.

"WHAT?!... Are you sure the news said that?" Desmond asked with a serious face and tightened jaw.

"Yes, that is exactly what they said. Matter of fact my girl Kenya called me and told me to turn to the news when they were talking about it and me and her was wondering who the shooter could be." Niya expressed.

"I can't believe this bullshit!" Desmond, bashed the counter with the side of his fist out of anger.

"But why would Shawn kill Excel and his son and shoot little Carlos?" Niya asked with a confused, disgusted face.

Desmond was enraged and struggling hard to hold his composure. He looked to his left and saw Carlos had walked into the kitchen. He looked more like his dad than ever.

"Hey y'all." Carlos said, easing his way to the fridge.

"Hey Lil Cuz." Desmond said, pissed the fuck off as he walked pass Carlos headed to his bedroom.

"What's wrong with Cousin Dez?" Carlos asked, paused in his tracks, wondering what was going on.

"It's just some stuff going on right now; everything will be okay though…I hope." Niya replied, giving Carlos a hug.

Desmond swiftly walked into his room and headed straight for the dresser. He took off his T-Shirt and tossed it to the side. He opened the drawer flipping through under clothes and socks and grabbed his gun holster and put it on. He flipped through the drawer once more and paused; scratching his head for a second and shut the drawer with a confused look on his face. Suddenly he remembered and walked over to the chest and opened the doors. He moved some stuff out of the way and saw his gun safe on the back shelf. He grabbed the safe and unlocked it with his thumb print. ***Yeah muthafucka,*** he uttered with a mean voice and took the gun out and sat the safe back in the chest. He looked and made sure Niya wasn't coming and then secured the gun in the holster down by his right side. He went in the closet and grabbed a short sleeve button up shirt. He just happened to look down and see an old picture of his Cousin Carlos Sr. and picked it up; the picture jogged his memory back to that last day he'd seen him. His nostrils flared and his jaw tightened as anger consumed his heart. He sat the picture down and put his shirt on; it perfectly concealed his pistol and he walked out the room. He walked downstairs knowing Niya would be seriously nervous and paranoid if she knew exactly what was on his mind. He walked in the kitchen and thought to himself this will be the perfect time to ease past Niya without her really questioning him about what he was about to go do because she was talking to Carlos Jr. He walked up to her and gave her a quick peck on the cheek ***I'll be right back in a moment.*** He grabbed his car keys off of the counter and headed for the door. Niya was caught up in her conversation with Carlos but slightly thrown off, wondering where Desmond was headed.

"Babe, where you going?" Niya asked Desmond, not trying to come across rude because Carlos was in the middle of saying something to her at the time.

"I gotta go holla at bro real quick; I'll be back." Desmond answered, managing to make his way out of the door without Niya questioning him and convincing him to stay.

Desmond hocked and spat on the ground as he looked around; he hated being watched. He got in his car and started it then turned on some hardcore music to ride to; War Ready by Rick Ross. Angered thoughts further fueled his rage and appetite for revenge as he drove through the city streets. He finally made his way over to Shawn's neck of the woods and turned down his block. He unsnapped the latch on his gun holster; quickly glancing in the rearview mirror. He vigilantly looked around at the neighbor's homes; no one really was outside or seemed to be paying attention. Unfortunately he didn't see Shawn's nor Marlo's car in the driveway as he calmly pulled up out front. He pulled a little further to see if any cars were parked back by the garage but saw that they weren't there. *Hmmm...* Desmond wondered where he could be and figured since he's always over his cousin's Ken Davis house he'd go see. He had to calm himself because he felt like he was about to start driving reckless through traffic; didn't need the police stopping him for speeding. He drove down West 6 Mile Rd for a while till he made it to Rosedale Park in Detroit where some of the more nicer homes and working class blacks live. He made a right turn on Rosemont Ave and cruised up a couple blocks. He peered closely at the houses till he recognized the house; still no sign of Shawn. He did see Ken's black GMC Terrain truck parked in the driveway so he decided to pay him a visit. He parked and quick glanced around the area; everything looked peaceful. He got out and walked up to the door and rang the doorbell. He glanced at his watch as he listened as someone was approaching the door.

"Hey, wsup good Bro!" Ken said joyously after opening the door and seeing that it was Desmond.

"Yo, wsup Bro, you alright?" Desmond answered, thinking of a reason to say why he stopped by.

"What brings you by?" Ken asked, unlocking the screen door and opening it.

"Man I need to use your bathroom bad." Desmond answered.

"All man, come on in; you already know where the bathroom is at." Ken said, opening the door.

"Bro, it's like everybody was outside so I couldn't like pull to the side and take a piss real quick without somebody seeing me." Desmond said, noticing that Ken was home alone.

"Oh hell no, the police have been patrolling the area kinda tuff lately; we had a couple break ins these last couple of weeks. And you do know that if police catch you pissing outside they're not just going to ticket you, but your name go on the sex offenders list." Ken said, going into the kitchen.

"Get the hell out of here! Are you serious?" Desmond asked, headed for the restroom.

"Serious as cancer." Ken answered, grabbing two crystal glasses from out of the kitchen cabinet.

Desmond went in the bathroom and took a piss; he hated the situation he is in and the measures he has to take to find Shawn. He zipped up his pants and shook his head as he looked at himself in the mirror while washing his hands. Ken is a cool humble dude that don't fuck with nobody and don't mind helping family and friends in need; however your relations and affiliations with individuals can be detrimental. Desmond exited the restroom and walked back into the dining room; Ken was opening a brand new fifth of Hennessy.

"You want some Hen, bro?" Ken asked, pouring himself a glass.

"Oh most definitely." Desmond replied.

Ken poured a nice double shot in Desmond's glass, they toasted and downed them.

"Aye, you heard from Shawn." Desmond asked as Ken poured them both another shot.

Ken was slightly caught off guard, but tried to play it off. He never liked speaking on Shawn nor his street life.

"Shawn? Psst I aint even heard from that fool." Ken answered, feeling awkward.

Desmond downed the hell out of his Hennessy; his head tilted all the way back. His shirt slightly raised brandishing his pistol on purpose. Sudden fear shot through Ken's stomach as his heart thumped harder. Desmond sat his glass on the table and looked Ken directly in the eyes. Ken's eyes were fixated on Desmond's gun and he looked up at him; it looked like he'd seen Medusa.

"Ken… Ima need you to tell me where Shawn is located and it's seriously important that you be very honest with me right now." Desmond said, looking at Ken with a straight face.

"Um…Uh…" Ken stuttered, barely getting his words together because he was scared.

"Ken, pour yourself another shot of Hennessey and down it right now; it'll help calm you and talk straight." Desmond said.

Ken's hand shook nervously as he poured himself another shot. He immediately downed the drink and sat the glass down. He slightly started to hyperventilate, trying to catch his breathe.

"KEN…where the fuck is Shawn at?" Desmond asked vehemently.

Ken didn't want to get killed and tried calming down best he could. "Okay, okay…look…wait a minute. I mean…I don't know exactly where Shawn is I swear. He was over here yesterday evening and he was talking about him leaving for New York to handle some business. I swear to you I didn't ask him about any names, locations, money, none of that shit. He asked me if I wanted some imported cigars and then he left. I swear that's all I know, Dez." Ken pleaded.

Desmond took a deep breath and stood there for a moment thinking. His eyes squinted as he pondered where the hell in New York could Shawn be. Then it came to him as he recalled Shawn talking about the cigars.

"You're a good guy Ken; I ain't never had no problems with you; you're alright with me. I just need you to do me a favor…" Desmond asked, glancing at the time on his watch.

"What's that?" Ken asked, nervous, just wishing Desmond would leave peacefully.

"This stays between me and you; matter of fact you haven't seen me in a while. We good on that?" Desmond asked.

"Yeah, yes we're definitely good on that; I give you my word on that." Ken nervously stuttered.

"Okay cool, I'm about to dip up out of here. Ken...please don't make me have to come holla at you." Desmond asked, looking him in the eye.

"I promise you, Dez; my word is gold. Me and Shawn ain't blood related anyway and I ain't got time for the drama. Don't want no parts of it no way no how." Ken assured.

"Cool, I'm out of here man; stay up." Desmond replied, headed to the door.

"Stay up? What does that mean?" Ken asked, fearing he was being threatened.

Desmond looked back at him. "It means just that; stay up, stay alive, be safe, that's all; I promise you it's not a threat Bro." Desmond assured and left out of the door.

Ken just shut the door behind him and exhaled deeply, shaking his head in disbelief. You never know the strength of terror till you've tasted it. Desmond glanced at his surroundings as he went and got in his car. He pulled off thinking to himself how the hell he was going to find this muthafucka quickly. Thoughts raced through his mind like crazy and then it came to him! He grabbed his phone and dialed his cousin Dax, up in Brooklyn New York. Dax had just finished interviewing a couple of talented young female artist on his radio talk show. He was still there conversing with them about having them back on the show. His cell phone vibrated so he glanced at it and saw that it was Desmond calling him. He wanted to shoot him to voicemail and call him back after he'd gotten done but he opted to excuse himself and step outside the studio to answer the call.

"Wsup Cousin? I'm literally wrapping up an interview on my talk show. Talk to me; what's good with you?" Dax asked.

"Well um damn, um I don't want to interrupt the show and fuck up the business so just call me when you get done." Desmond replied.

"Nall go ahead and shoot it to me real quick, I got a second or two. Is everything okay?" Dax asked, lightly tugging on his beard.

"Well, I'ma just keep it straight to the point; Shawn and Timothy killed Excel, his son, and shot little Carlos." Desmond answered.

Dax was thrown the fuck off and eased his way down the hallway for a little privacy. "Okay hold the fuck up. What the fuck did I just hear you say?" Dax asked with a serious look on his face.

"Well police did an investigation and picked up Timothy. Timothy dropped a dime on Shawn and now police is looking for his ass now (duplicate). I just drove past that niggas house and he nor his woman was there. Then I went to his cousin's house and kind of showed my pistol and scared the info out of him." Desmond replied.

"So did he tell you where he at?" Dax asked with a mean scowl on his face.

"Yeah, his ass headed up to New York yesterday. His cousin told me that Shawn told him he was coming up there to holla at his guy at a cigar joint." Desmond answered.

"What?!" Dax asked, looking around, hoping no one heard him getting loud.

"Yup, that's what he told me. Fucked up thing about it is I don't know the name of the joint; I forgot." Desmond replied.

"Well if it's that one I think I recall him speaking on before then that's right here in Brooklyn." Dax replied, balling his fist tightly with an angered face.

"Damn, I wish I could get my hands on him right now." Desmond replied.

"Don't worry, the shit gone get handled. I'm just trippin that this muthafucka even have the nerve to kill my cousin and feel comfortable coming to my home! Oh yeah I promise you I'm about to show him how we get down in Brook Town; Word to God!" Dax said emphatically!

Tracking

The manhunt was on; the detectives worked diligently to find Shawn ASAP. Detective Valencia was on the case looking through Facebook to find his profile. They were looking for any and everything that could lead to his whereabouts. Timothy also told them about Shawn's woman Marlo. When she pulled up Shawn's page she immediately saw where he was in a relationship with Marlo and she clicked on her page. Detective Melvin walked up swiftly ***Okay tell me something good.*** Detective Valencia transferred her computer screen to the jumbo monitor up on the wall for the team to see. She went back on Shawn's page and pulled up his Facebook page. Officer Jeff and other officers assigned to the team had their note pads and ink pens jotting down details. They had his full name, age, date of birth, and the city and state he lives in. They went through a variety of his pictures and took note of his build, his tattoos, his facial hair, pictures without his facial hair etc. They also noticed pictures of him posting large amounts of weed, money, various cigars domestic and imported. Detective Melvin watched with an eagle eye as Detective Valencia scrolled various pictures.

"Hold on! Click on that picture right there." Detective Melvin said, pointing.

"Which one?" Detective Valencia asked.

"The one right there with him in the white shirt and black hat. Yes that one, blow that one up for me." Detective Melvin said.

Detective Valencia blew the picture up and noticed a gun that was brandished on his side. She decided to blow the picture up larger. "Wait a minute. Is that the same gun used to kill Peaches and DeYonte?"

"It damn sure looks like it. Save that picture and let's see if he's posted any recent statuses maybe telling us where he's at or where he's headed." Detective Melvin said.

Detective Valencia clicked back onto his profile page and scrolled his statuses.

"He hasn't posted anything in the last few days." Detective Valencia said.

"Click on his woman's page let's see what this Ms. Marlo is about." Detective Melvin said.

Detective Valencia clicked on her page and began scrolling. She tilted her head as she noticed a picture Marlo had posted of Shawn not too long ago. He was leaned up against the back of a car posing for the picture.

"Hello!" Detective Valencia said, hyped that they found a very good lead.

"Hell yeah! Jeff run a trace on that license plate and post the picture on our Crime Catcher's website and see what we find." Detective Melvin said.

"Let's see where the post was made from." Detective Valencia said, clicking on the picture.

"Damn no location. Aye wait a second; zero in on the name of the gas station and street signs behind it at the light pole." Detective Melvin said.

Detective Valencia blew up the picture and got the name of the gas station and the cross streets. Officer Thomas looked up the name of the gas station and the streets on his phone immediately.

"Sir, this gas station is located in Brooklyn New York." Officer Thomas said.

"Brooklyn New York? Officer Carter I need you to get on the phone with the New York police department right now." Detective Melvin said.

"Yes sir." Officer Latrice Carter replied.

"I need this joker bagged today." Detective Melvin said with a mean look on his face and his arms folded as he stared at Shawn's picture.

"This dude is good as got." Detective Valencia said, looking back at Detective Melvin.

Let Us Prey

It has been said that death comes in threes…

Brooklyn New York - A 2018 Dodge Durango pulled up in front of the Cigar Express. The passenger back door opened and a cocky dark skinned dude stepped out with a grimacing look on his face. The driver got out and looked around and scanned the surroundings. He took one more toke on his cigarette and thumped it in the street. Smoke exhaled from his mouth as he walked around the other side of the truck. The passenger door opened and Dax got out. His dark shades concealed the anger in his eyes. He shut the door and they pulled out their guns as they headed inside. The guy who runs the shop was inside straightening the shelves and never noticed the truck pull up out front. He heard someone come in and turned around to greet his customers. ***Hello, welcome to Cigar Express.*** His eyes lit up like high beams and fear succumbed him immediately. He started backing up with his hands up, bumping up against the counter. ***Please don't kill me! You can have the money, all of it; just don't kill me.***

"Where the fuck is Shawn at?" Dax asked aggressively.

"Shawn?" Germaine asked.

"Nigga, don't make me send you to the afterlife! I've already been put up on game that muthafucka was coming here to do business with you! Now again where the fuck is Shawn at?!!" Dax asked, stepping around the counter.

"Bro please, don't shoot. Shawn just left here about an hour ago!" Germaine answered, petrified as fuck.

"Dog…you know what?" Dax asked, cocking his pistol and aiming it at Germaine.

Germaine instinctively jumped on the floor with his hands up trembling in a blocking position.

"NO, NO, NO Please wait, he said something about him and his girl going over to some bar; Black Star Bar or something like that. I swear that's all I know man." Germaine answered.

"Dog, you better not be lying…matter of fact; gimme your I.D. now." Dax asked, aiming his pistol at him again.

Germaine's hand was shaking like a rattlesnake as he carefully reached in his back pocket to grab his wallet. He was so scared as he handed his wallet to Dax. Dax sat his pistol down on the glass counter full of humidors and cigars. He opened the wallet and took his I.D. out. He sat the wallet down on the counter and placed Germaine's I.D. in his pocket. Dax looked at his fellas and said ***Let's head to Black Star.*** Dax and both his goons turned around and headed out the door. Germaine just sat there on the floor and then abruptly reached in his pocket and grabbed his cellphone. His hand was lightly shaking from nervousness. He swiftly went to his contacts and pulled up Shawn's name. Something caught his attention and he looked behind himself. It was the big fella standing there with the gun barrel pointed at his face as he pulled the trigger.

Black Star Bar

Black Star bar was a nice size bar; it wasn't the greatest but it wasn't a hole in the wall either. On this day it was a fairly decent crowd, they were chill and listening to music. Marlo sat at the bar sipping her liquor while looking at the Detroit Pistons game. Out her peripheral she could see guys constantly staring at her ass hanging over the bar stool but she paid them no mind. She already had her mind set on a dude at the other end of the bar who had been eyeing her and had sent her a couple of drinks already. She sized him up from top to bottom; from his hair cut, to his designer shirt, jeans and shoes. She figured he might have been a baller, or got a really good job however she saw dollar signs. They shared mutual attraction as far as looks were concerned but their agendas were totally different. He saw a fine ass chick that he would love to holla at, get to know or at least fuck. She saw a possible candidate she could get close to and possibly set him up to get jacked for his money. She received a text from Shawn downstairs telling her to bring him a double shot of Patron. She got the bartenders attention and ordered the drink and noticed the guy she had her eye on approaching her. He stepped to her with an easing smile on his face.

"Hey, excuse me beautiful. How are you?" Kevin asked, extending his hand for a pleasant handshake.

"Thank you handsome, I'm okay and you?" Marlo asked, shaking his hand.

"I'm fine baby. What's your name?" Kevin asked.

"Candace." Marlo answered.

"Candace, I like that; my name is Kevin." Kevin replied, noticing she had finished the drink she had.

"Nice to meet you, Kevin." Marlo replied.

"So what's a beautiful lady like you doing here all by herself?" Kevin asked.

Marlo smirked "Technically, I'm not here by myself."

"Oh, well I aint trying to step on nobody's toes or nothing. I just think you're sexy as ever and wanted to try to get to know you." Kevin replied, hoping she gives him her number anyway.

"Nall, you good, it ain't even like that." Marlo replied.

Kevin got the bartenders attention real quick.

"Hey, what can I get for you?" The bartender asked.

"I want to open another tab and get another round for this beautiful lady right here and myself." Kevin answered.

"Okay so that'll be a Hennessy straight up on the rocks for you and another Tequila Sunrise for the beautiful lady?" The bartender asked.

"Yes." Kevin answered, handing the bartender his Visa Black Card.

"Is that okay for you?" The bartender asked, looking at Marlo.

"Yes, thank you." Marlo answered, briefly noticing what type of credit card he had and looked away.

Kevin looked back at her thinking damn she is fine. "Well I really don't know exactly what you got going on but maybe we can exchange numbers and talk about it one day over the phone." Kevin suggested.

"That's no problem." Marlo replied.

"That aint gone cause no issues for you will it?" Kevin asked.

"No not at all." Marlo replied.

"Your beautiful self probably aint gone even call me." Kevin said, hoping she would assure him she would.

"Yes, I'm going to call you tomorrow and maybe we can have a fun conversation over breakfast one day." Marlo replied.

The bartender returned "Here's you guys drinks."

"Thank you." Kevin said to the bartender.

"You want me to keep the tab open?" The bartender asked.

"Yes." Kevin answered.

"Thank you." Marlo said, looking at Kevin.

"Any time, gorgeous." Kevin replied, holding his glass up to toast with her.

"To meeting new people and the good life." Marlo replied, touching glasses with his.

Now downstairs in the basement Shawn and a few fellas were playing a serious game of spades. It was Shawn and his partner Robert, and then Daniel and his partner Harold. There was alcohol and money on the table; fifteen dollars a hand so of course there was no room for all that playing for fun shit. It had been a very competitive game going back and forth but Shawn and his partner was winning and damn near up two-hundred dollars. The other fellas was feeling the pressure because they were losing money. Robert dealt the hand while Shawn was texting Marlo.

How we looking up there? Shawn asked as he hit send.

Immediately Marlo text back "We looking real good right about now."

"We got one to go?" Shawn asked, gathering his hand together and putting his suits in order.

"Hell yeah, and he's a spender; easy money." Marlo replied.

"Cool, I'll be up there in a little bit. Ima bust these niggas ass for a few more hands and get the rest of their money and we out." Shawn replied, sitting his phone down and glancing over at Daniel and Harold.

"Who it's on?" Shawn asked, sipping his liquor.

"It's on me to bid." Daniel answered, glancing at Harold just over the edge of his cards.

The waitress approached the table with a drink that Daniel ordered. ***Here's your Gentleman's Jack you ordered***. Daniel pulled out some money and paid her along with a tip. He sat his drink to the side and put his money back in his pocket. He reopened his hand and glanced over at Harold. Shawn figured he was cheating and couldn't believe this nigga. He couldn't believe he was actually trying to do that shit right in front of his face.

"Yo dog, for real, money? We doing it like that now?" Shawn asked, looking over at Daniel with a snarl on his face.

Daniel looked at Shawn "What you talking about, bruh?"

"Dog, you looking over at Harold trying to look for a sign when you supposed to be bidding." Shawn pointed out, starting to get heated.

"Dog, aint nobody trying to cheat on you, nigga." Daniel replied.

"You know what dog, check this the fuck out; ain't none of that looking over the fucking table shit when we got fucking money on muthafuckin the table, flat the fuck out." Shawn said, repeatedly slapping the table along with every word he spoke.

"Dog, like I said ain't nobody trying to cheat you bruh; just play the game." Daniel said, cutting him off.

"Nall, fuck that, game over; get the fuck up off the table." Shawn said, grabbing the money they had in the pot on the table and putting it in his pocket.

Harold saw it was starting to get hostile and tried to defuse the situation. "Aye y'all chill man."

"Nall nigga, fuck chill; you the one brought this hoe ass nigga over here." Shawn retorted.

"Nigga, put my money back on the table before we have a problem." Daniel said, standing up.

Shawn scooted back in his chair and lifted the right side of his shirt brandishing his pistol. "Muthafucka you already got problems, nigga. Don't get finalized up in this bitch trying to be hard, nigga. Look around you playboy; trust me today ain't your lucky day." Shawn stressed.

Daniel noticed the dudes at the pool table had stopped playing. They'd sat their pool sticks down on the pool table; looking at Daniel while cracking their knuckles and ready to beat his ass. Daniel looked at Harold and Harold just shook his head because it was out of his hands.

"Aye nigga, run them pockets." Shawn said, looking at Daniel in his eyes.

"Huh?" Daniel replied, caught off guard; thinking he should try and run.

Shawn immediately got up, grabbing his gun and got in Daniel's face. "Nigga, don't huh me, I said run them muthafuckin pockets."

Shawn aggressively reached inside of Daniel's front pocket like he was a little rag doll and pulled out a lil knott of money. He looked at the money and said ***Okay now where even,*** and stuffed it in his pocket. He reached inside of his other front pocket and pulled out Daniel's wallet.

He opened it up and took out his I.D. ***Yeah, this here is for insurance purposes just in case you wanna get stupid I know how to get at you.*** Shawn reached down and grabbed Daniel's drink off of the table that he had just ordered and downed it. ***Man, how do you drink this nasty ass shit? Get the fuck out of this basement.*** Daniel felt completely hoe'd out, humiliated and robbed of all manhood. Daniel wasn't no hoe ass nigga but his heart raced fearfully; unknowing if he would be ambushed from behind. His breathing started getting tight as he approached the top of the stairwell. He was an asthmatic and needed to sit down to catch his breath. Some stared at him as he made his way to the bar and sat down. The bartender noticed the troubled looking man as he sat down and walked over to him.

"Would you like something to drink?" The bartender asked, grabbing a food menu and placing it in front of Daniel.

"No I'm straight." Daniel replied, shaking his head looking off out of the front window of the bar.

"Alright let me know if you need anything." The bartender replied.

Daniel immediately retorted. "Hey, hey excuse me, yeah I'll take a ice water and a Gentleman's Jack."

"Okay, I'll be right back." The bartender answered.

"Hey wait, I forgot my dumb ass don't have any money. Scratch the jack and let me get an ice water." Daniel replied, looking up at the TV screen mounted up over the bar checking out the ESPN Highlights.

"I'll tell you what, you look like you can use a drink right now. Don't worry about it; the Jack is on the house." The bartender replied and went to make his drink.

The bartender went to go make his drink and at that point Daniel looked back at the TV screen with and incredulous face. He couldn't believe what he was seeing; breaking news; there was a nationwide manhunt for Shawn. Daniel figured this was the perfect way to get back at that nigga. He immediately took his cell phone out of its holster and dialed the anonymous number on the screen. He provided the police with the information they needed from description to location. The bartender returned with Daniel's drink ***Thank you, I appreciate that.*** Daniel smirked as he sipped his drink; he stared at Marlo walking out of the bathroom and went and sat back down next to ole boy at the bar. He glanced back at the TV screen and watched a rerun game of Brooklyn Nets verses the Detroit Pistons. Shortly after Shawn emerged from the basement. He'd caught Marlo's attention and nodded his head like let's go. He stepped outside and lit him a cigarette; he blew the smoke out as he looked around to see what he could see. ***Fuck*** Shawn uttered noticing the police coming up the block. ***What's wrong?*** Marlo asked, wondering what Shawn was looking at. ***Police coming up the block so let's go ahead and leave; just act normal.*** They were parked just out front so they wasted no time getting in the car and pulling off. The police had noticed Shawn getting into the car and pulling off so they accelerated. Shawn glanced in his rearview mirror and sped up and bent the corner; he had a gut feeling that something wasn't right. He looked in his rearview mirror again and saw the squad cars aggressively bending that corner. There was no doubt in his mind that the NYPD was chasing him. At this point he had nothing to lose; it was either natural life behind bars, death, or freedom. Shawn bent another corner and really put the petal to the floor. He whipped up the streets weaving through tight traffic. ***Oh***

my God, Oh my God, Oh my God Marlo yelled, clinching the door handle tightly hoping he doesn't crash. He repeatedly blew his horn as he violently sped through busy intersections with stop signs. Marlo started to panic more and more with every near miss. She prayed and vowed she'd never set anyone else up or harm anyone if God just help her make it through this alive. Shawn quickly glanced in his rearview mirror, ***Damn I can't shake these bitches.*** Shawn thought real quickly as he approached a main busy intersection. The light had been green for a moment; he knew it was about to turn red. He saw the light turn yellow and accelerated; just before he got there it turned red. He quickly glanced both ways as he entered the intersection and gunned it. Marlo's eyes were wide and written with terror. ***SHAWNNNNN*** Marlo screamed as she noticed a Black Dodge Ram pickup truck speeding along the far side. ***FUCK*** Shawn yelled, beeping his horn like a mad man looking in the opposite direction. The passenger window shattered flying everywhere as they got T-boned. The car spun three-sixty out of control; you could hear the tires squeal across the asphalt. The driver's side door slammed hard as fuck into the light pole causing Shawn to bang his head. The car finally stopped as they slid up on the sidewalk. Marlo was so damn dizzy; slowly blinking trying to regain focus. She saw smoke rise from the hood through the cracked windshield. People that were in the corner gas station and other surrounding businesses came out to see the commotion. A few people pulled out their cell phones and started recording the action. One of them was actually live streaming everything on Facebook. Marlo glanced over at Shawn; he seemed to be losing consciousness. He was in an awkward position from the slightly smashed in driver's side door. His left arm and hand were numb from the impact; unsuccessfully he kept trying to unfasten his seat belt with a weak effort. Several white police officers approached aggressively with their guns drawn. ***PUT YOUR HANDS UP WHERE I CAN SEE THEM.*** Marlo put her hands up and yelled ***HE'S INJURED; HE CAN BARELY MOVE.*** Shawn tried his best to turn around and the officer fired four rounds directly into Shawn's chest making sure he killed him. Marlo screamed for her life yet she kept her hands raised. She put her hands out the window making it clear she didn't have a weapon. ***KEEP YOUR HANDS UP*** the second officer yelled trying to intimidate her. If she would've blinked wrong he would've exterminated her gladly. He roughly opened up the car door and snatched her out, throwing her to the ground. She automatically put her hands behind her back so his sorry ass couldn't yell stop resisting and shoot her like they did Alston. He put his fat ass knee in her back trying to hurt her. He grabbed for his handcuffs with one hand and his gun still aimed at her in his other hand. Another officer ran up yelling ***STAY ON THE GROUND*** knowing all along she wasn't even moving and mashed his knee in her lower back hurting her lower spine. The officer noticed he was already being video recorded so he couldn't pretend she was resisting arrest and just shoot her. The shooting officer saw that he was being recorded and put on a fake ass charade like he felt regret for killing Shawn by yelling ***FUCK…FUCK…FUCK.*** Blood spilled out of Shawn's mouth as he died trying to put his hands up.

RELATIONSHIP AND FAMILY REJUVENATION

Friday – February 7th, 2020 – Artist Village – Detroit-Michigan - 7pm. It was a beautiful day for families and couples in relationships. Family, Relationship, and Love Rejuvenation conference was taking place. Plenty people were in attendance and the energy in the air was exuberant. The idea of the conference was to inspire positivity, love, and strength back into our families and relationships. A wonderful lady by the name Kim Carter was the host and was one of the people who helped put on the event. The crowd applauded as the woman who just finished speaking exited the stage. Kim Carter walked back up on the stage to engage the crowd. ***Yall keep it going for Mrs. Sarah Langston.*** The crowd applauded once again as she took center stage. ***Now how powerful was that?! That was some very, very insightful information from a well respected lady in our community. I hope yall enjoying yourselves as much as I am because we don't get positive relationship strengthening information like this on the regular. We get all of the negative, disheartening bull crap bombarded on us twenty-four seven from television, music, internet, social media, our inbox etc. Oh yes don't get me started on this***

inbox drama. The crowd very much applauded when she mentioned inbox drama. ***The next person I'm bringing to the stage is a very good friend of mine and therapist Ms. Niya Chapman.*** The crowd applauded as Niya walked up on the stage. The pressure of the moment felt heavy as she stepped in front of the microphone. She took a deep breath, exhaled and looked out at the crowd. ***Good evening everyone; I'm honored to be here and share my thoughts with you all. I'm really big on our relationships and families becoming stronger and lasting. Having our children grow up in positive two parent homes like all children should. I love the way this organization is set up because it focuses on the pros and cons of both parties in the relationship. It teaches us the importance of understanding one another, how to heal, be caring, loving and cater to each other's needs. One key ingredient that is imperative to holding our relationships and families together is having honor...having honor for your mate, having honor for your marriage, having honor for your children, having honor for you family... I say that because we take pride and care for what we have honor for. That honor is like the armor and shield of your relationships and marriages. And today in Twenty-twenty we need that honor more than ever because we live in a toxic society that destroys relationships and marriages with ease... Some of our young girls have been preprogrammed by hurt mother's that all men are just dogs. Some of our young boys have been preprogrammed by their father's that women are just gold diggers and good for sex only. So much toxicity in television, radio, social media and that all mighty inbox... I just recently lost a dear friend who really could've benefited from this conference. She was beautiful and ambitious just like some of you in the audience. She was vibrant, she was funny and had just got engaged to be married. And just like many of us she had***

some stumbling blocks in her relationship except her story ended in a fatal love triangle. Her and her man decided they needed space as they tried to reconcile their issues. In the process she hooked up with her ex and things happened and she regretted it afterwards. Her and her man decided to reconcile and make the relationship work. They ended up getting engaged and she was happier than she had ever been in her life. She wore her ring like a medal of honor and shut down anyone who didn't respect that. Unfortunately her new Fiancé stumbled upon her open Facebook page and looked in her inbox. That's when he discovered a message sent to her by her ex stating that he'd given her A.I.D.S. Her Fiancé then orchestrated her death, her ex's death and took his own life. And with that being said if anyone is in a relationship and you have a good mate treat them right. And definitely keep the drama out of your inbox. Niya finished her speech and exited the stage. She smiled as the crowd applauded her for her very touching story. She exhaled, thinking to herself how glad she was to have gotten that off her chest. Ever since Peaches passed she had be motivated to speak at domestic violence seminars and to couples. She was honored and saluted for her motivating words. She smiled as she saw Desmond standing up clapping and smiling as she approached.

"Babe you sounded absolutely beautiful and heartfelt up there." Desmond said.

"Did I? Thank you honey." Niya said, hugging him and kissing him.

"I'm proud of you sweetie; you touched a lot of people with your words." Desmond smiled.

"You think so?" Niya asked, looking up at him.

"I know so." Desmond replied.

By this time Tangie was walking up accompanied with her niece.

"Bravo, bravo, bravo, girl you did an excellent job up there." Tangie said.

"Hey, I'm so glad you made it. I wasn't sure if you showed up." Niya replied.

"Oh I wasn't missing this." Tangie said, hugging Niya.

"And who is this beautiful young lady you have with you?" Niya asked, smiling.

"This is my younger cousin DeRay who I wanted to hear you speak. I thought it would be great for her to hear." Tangie answered.

"Hi DeRay, nice to meet you; so glad you could come." Niya said, giving DeRay a hug.

"Thank you I really enjoyed your speech." DeRay said, smiling.

"Thank you so much." Niya replied.

"I really needed to hear that. Some of the things you said actually felt like you were talking directly to me." DeRay said, glancing at her phone because it was ringing.

"Well I'm definitely honored that I was able to touch you with my words and hopefully it makes a difference in a very positive way." Niya replied.

"Um can you excuse me I have to take this call?" DeRay asked, answering her phone.

DeRay excused herself from the conversation as she quickly headed to the hallway with the phone to her ear.

"Hello, what's up?" DeRay said, stepping out of the auditorium and shutting the door behind her.

"Aye, you still coming this way?" Duran asked.

"Yes, I'll be there; I'm still at the seminar." DeRay answered, flicking hair out of her eye.

"Okay, see you when you get here Sweetie." Duran replied.

"Okay." DeRay hung up the phone and exhaled.

DeRay shook her head and reached in her purse and pulled out a vape pen. She looked around to see if anyone was looking and then took a good puff. She exhaled a thick cloud of vapors. She put her phone on selfie video mode and tapped the record icon. She held the phone up in front of her face as she stared at the screen batting her eyelashes. She took another puff from her vape Pen again and exhaled a cloud of vapors at the phone. She ended the video and posted it on Facebook. Immediately her alerts started going off from people liking her video to inbox messages. She opened up her messages with an incredulous look on her face. It was another dick pick; nothing she's not used to. She looked at the name of the sender again; it read ***Doughboy.***

The End.

Here's a sneak peek at my next novel titled

INbOX 2 Gender War

The light sound of snoring came from her wide opened mouth. The night crept upon as she laid there on the couch napping for hours. Her body slightly twitched, perhaps whatever she was dreaming of she was trying to wake up from. She started breathing through her nostrils the more she came to. She winced with a bitter face as she slowly blinked her eyes; the living room was dark. She reached to her right patting around eventually grabbing her cellphone. Her eyes squinted from the bright light as she dialed the number. She put it on speaker phone and it went straight to voice-mail. ***The person you're trying to reach has a voice-mail that has not been set up yet, goodbye.*** She ended the call and went on her Facebook page. Nothing new, just a bunch of random post from her friends. One particular post stood out from one of her LGBTQ friends. She thought to herself ***Yall still trolling***

Dave Chapelle? It's been months now; leave that man alone. She continued scrolling, eventually going to her friends list and went to his page. She saw a post he made hours ago, clicked a heart on it. Then clicked on the message tab. ***Hey babe wya? I called you; call me back when you get this...***

...Breathe

February 2021 – 11:49 pm. The streets never looked more frozen and frigid. The concrete looked so cold you might break a bone just daydreaming of landing on it the wrong way. She squinted her eyes trying to see the dark figure walking across the road ahead of her as she drove up 6 Mile Rd approaching Gratiot Ave. Half the streetlights barely work; best lighting you get is when cars drive by. It just seems everything and everyone is so void of love. The homeless slept slumped over in bus stops that reeked of piss and alcohol. She shook her head, ***Wow, how do they survive through the winter like this? No food, no heat, no family...Bless them lord.*** The sound of gospel music played as she sung along passionately. She drummed her fingertips on the steering wheel during the epic drum breakdown in the song. She started rocking back and forth as she made it to his street and turned. ***Bless me lord, I'm changing; I want to do better.*** She slowed up in front of his house and turned the music down. She parked and grabbed her phone and dialed his number. It rang four times and went to his voice-mail. She sniffled as she looked up at the windows in his house and dialed his number once again. This time it rung once and went straight to voice-mail. Her hand trembled even more as her nervousness and emotions started getting the best of her. ***So you can't answer the damn phone?*** She questioned her beliefs and if there was a God. Her thoughts activated her anxiety, psychosis and nervousness. Tears streamed down her face as she rocked back and forth and scratched the steering wheel. The moment felt so surreal ***Am I dreaming? Why is this happening to Meeeeeeeee!*** She felt like she was repeating the same steps over and over in her mind. She called his phone once again and it went straight to voice-mail. ***Dammit I need you; I can't breathe right!... I'm scared. I'm not cooperative; I mean I am cooperative. Why is this happening to me? Am I going crazy? No, I'm not crazy, I'm not crazy, I'm not CRAZY!*** There was a brief silence as she tried to gather her thoughts. She closed her eyes and slowed her breathing down; this always helped her with her panic attacks. She called his phone again and got his voice-mail. ***Answer the phoneeeee! Answer the fucking phone!*** She had a small personal double shot of liquor in her middle console. She took it out, twisted the cap off and downed all of it. That shot wasn't enough so she roughly fumbled through the console searching for another shot. She felt a cylinder bottle and paused for a second. She shook the bottle and from the rattle she knew it was her prescription she hadn't been taking... Haventeral. She looked at herself in the rearview mirror as she pulled it out. Then slowly opened it and took out a tablet and placed it in her mouth. She had a little bottled water left sitting there and took a swig. She slowly took out another pill and placed it in her mouth and then abruptly dumped the rest of the bottle in her mouth. She swallowed the rest of the water and grabbed her revolver off the passenger seat. She sat there spinning the barrel and thinking. ***He needs to answer the phone...I...am...COOPERATIVE.***

Here's another sneak peek at my up and coming novel titled...

ROOT

The Pursuit of Love Forbidden

4:37 pm – Saturday – April 1st, 2023 – The weather felt brisk outside, a chilly day; sixty-one degrees with cloudy skies. Wind chimes made melody on the front porch as the wind blew. Inside the home was various ornaments that represented spirituality from dream catchers to candles. Statues of Demigods and Hindu Prayer Offerings adorned the mantle piece and other places throughout the house. The scent of sage burned from room to room as the breeze blew through the front door. Momma Ava kept her house very clean as she swept in her dining room. Her house was old fashion and always felt cozy and welcoming. She could hear foot steps up her wooden front porch and a knock at her front door. ***Just a second*** she said as she sat her broom against the wall and walked to the front door.

"Welcome, welcome, welcome my dear friend, how are you?" Momma Ava asked, unlocking the front door and opening it.

"I'm fantastic Momma Ava. How are you?" He answered, stepping inside and receiving a huge meaningful hug.

"I'm fine my love. Come on in the kitchen and have a seat; I have some hot water heating on the stove for us some tea." Momma Ava said, stepping through the long drape of beads as you step in the kitchen.

"Oh yes, I love your tea and your house is always so therapeutic. I just feel so relaxed whenever I come over here." He said, stepping through the beads and having a seat at the kitchen table.

"Thank you, I take much pride in having a house of love and positive energy." Momma Ava replied, looking towards the stove as the tea pot whistled.

"And please don't take offense but I love the old wall paper that you have on your kitchen walls after all of these years. I just love that retrospect type of feeling." He said, looking around the kitchen.

"Ah yes it gives you that feeling of stepping back in time a little bit. This was my mother's old house passed down to me before she died; she was very spiritual." Momma Ava said, grabbing to coffee cups from the cabinet.

"Well if she was anything like you, she was a very beautiful and I see where you get it from." He said, as she poured the hot water in the cups.

"Thank you, yes she was very sweet and deep in the power of good energy and magic." Momma Ava replied.

"Wow that's beautiful." He replied.

"The sugar, honey, lemons, tea bags and spoons are right there on the table already." Momma Ava said, sitting the cups down on the table.

"This is perfect." He said, grabbing his spoon and making his tea.

"Well what is this strong love energy I feel radiating from you?" Momma Ava asked, sitting down and bouncing her tea bag in her cup.

"Well.... there's a lady I am highly attracted to mentally and physically. She's thirty-seven or eight, and she's beautiful with this gorgeous smile. She has beautiful hair, the perfect shape, she's funny, she's smart I mean I can go on and on about why I adore her." He said, sipping his tea.

"Wow she sounds pretty amazing." Momma Ava replied, adding honey to her tea and stirring it.

"Amazing is an understatement; this woman is absolutely astounding." He replied.

"Okay well how did you meet this lovely lady?" Momma Ava asked.

"Well I always had a really big crush on her back when she was in middle school and high school. After she graduated, we kind of lost contact until one day on social media I saw her page and sent her a friend request. I messaged her often and we have some really good conversations about our lives and the things we're into." He answered.

"Well have you two dated?" Momma Ava asked.

"No....That's where I need your help." He answered.

"Oh you need like some advice on how to approach her?" Momma Ava asked.

"Hmmm...it's a little bit deeper than that." He answered.

"Okay so what's the obstacle that's keeping you from going to get your dream girl?" momma Ava asked.

"Dream girl, hmmm?... yeah...I like that. She is my dream girl." He said, nodding his head and thinking deeply.

"Well what's stopping you?" She asked.

"Her husband." He answered, sipping his tea.

"Husband?" Momma Ava asked with a straight face.

"Or husband to be, I forget." He added.

"Husband to be? Fiancé?" She asked, eyebrow raised.

"Yes, but truthfully I know I'm the husband she really supposed to be with." He answered.

"Does she know how you feel about her?" Momma Ava asked.

"I'm sure she knows I like her but I don't know if she knows just how much I like her. Like…what I'm willing to do to have her in my life." He replied.

"So what is it that you wish to do?" Momma Ava asked.

"Well I purchased these books and I did a little research and that's what led me to you… I want you to help me put a root on her." He said.

Momma Ava eased back a little, and looked at him with deep thought written in her eyes. Tapping into the spiritual world is no joking game.

"You do know rooting someone is a very deep and powerful energy? Summoning spiritual energy on someone against their will can turn out to be very detrimentally Karmic on the one summoning the root." Momma Ava sincerely expressed.

"I'm not worried about that; I just need to do it. How much do you charge?" He asked, pulling out his wallet.

"Um…I can't…I don't do that anymore." Momma Ava answered.

"Please? I need this." He said, placing two-hundred dollars on the table.

"I'm sorry but I can't." Momma Ava answered, sliding his money back.

"I need this…" He said sincerely, placing three-hundred more dollars on the table and sliding it to her.

Momma Ava took a deep breath. She looked at him with her strong eyes for a moment. She looked at the money and took it. She got up from the table and walked to the kitchen cabinet. She pulled out some spices such as Black Pepper, Cayenne Pepper, Jolokia Pepper, Habanero

Pepper, Cascarilla powder, Cochicowcow powder, salt, and a few other spices that create heat and sat them on the table. She went to the refrigerator and grabbed a lemon. She walked to the counter and grabbed one small white bag and one small black bag from out of the drawer. She grabbed a piece of paper and pencil out of another drawer and a sharp knife from the other drawer. She sat down at the table and placed everything before her. She pulled out a lighter and lit a candle. She tore two small pieces of paper and sat them before him with the pencil.

"Write the complete names of both people you wish to separate; one on one paper and one on the other paper." Momma Ava said.

She took the knife and slit the lemon in half as he wrote the names. Then with the tip of the knife she hollowed each side of the lemon out carefully. She added a pinch of each spice inside each half of the lemon. She took one of the names and stuffed it in the lemon, placing it inside one of the bags and twisting it so the name wouldn't come out. She took the other name and did the same thing with the other half of the lemon and bag.

"You will carefully take each one of these lemons and get rid of them far apart from each other. Just make sure you do it at least a few blocks from here." Momma Ava stated.

"No problem Momma Ava and thank you so much." He replied, getting up out of his chair.

"Oh and one more thing..." Momma Ava, walking to the kitchen cabinet.

"Yes Momma Ava?" He asked.

She flipped through a few vials and grabbed the one she was looking for. She shut the cabinet doors and walked over to him.

"Preferably after they break up you have to place four droplets of this in her drink. After that she'll find you irresistible and come for you."

"Thank you so much Momma Ava. I'm definitely going to get my dream girl."

"Just remember, there's no turning back now...and Karma is absolute." Momma Ava reminded him.

He couldn't wait to get home and put his plan into action. Momma Ava could see that he was eager or better yet desperate to will her into his world. But...something about his spirit didn't sit easy with her. Her eyes squinted as she sipped her tea and just before he could leave she stopped him.

"Hey, one more thing."

He turned around and smiled feeling happy. "Yes mam."

"I just want to tell you that you have a presence about you." Momma Ava said, very concerned.

He winced and his eyes fluttered. "I've felt that feeling periodically. My Ex told me it was her grandmother."

Momma Ava paused for a second...and responded. "That was not her Grandmother."

To be continued...

Thank You to all of my readers and supporters. I would like to share a bit more about myself that you may not know. I am a cool down to earth brotha who grew up in Detroit Michigan. I started off rappin in a group called Low Life. As I got older and my daughter was born I gravitated to poetry where I found my voice and purpose once again. My stage name is Men-Tal and recently I took on the alter alias Pen Writes.